Keith Gray's exploration of an invisible sub-culture hits you so hard it almost hurts. It has the power and realism to grip the reader and lead you into a dark, underground world of emotional outcasts.
DAMIAN KELLE

WAREHOUSE is **Keith Gray** on finest form, and doing what he does best: giving voices to the underdogs.
CHRIS WOODING

The **warehouse** is: 'the somewhere else you can go when there's nowhere else left.' Located in the dockland of a small northern town, the warehouse is a refuge for young people who have slipped through society's safety net. A cast of memorable characters - Robbie, Amy, Kinard, Lem and Canner - have, for various reasons found themselves there. They face a struggle for survival, but for dignity too. In a skillfully-constructed three-part narrative **Keith Gray** has produced a fast-paced, convincing and moving story. Keith's shorter fiction is some of the best around. This terrific book shows that he has just as much to say to older readers. **WAREHOUSE** deserves the widest readership.
ALAN GIBBONS

A brilliant, on-the-edge adventure into a secret world-within-the-world of teenage outsiders. **WAREHOUSE** is gutsy, gripping, dangerous, tender and real. **Keith Gray** delves into teen life in offbeat ways that no one else thinks of. This is strong, authentic fiction that gets right to the heart of what it feels like to be young, now.

JULIE BERTAGNA

WAREHOUSE is about many things. It's about the inequality of life. It's about bad luck, that capricious wind of change which so swiftly torpedoes expectations and potential. It's about evil people. But it's also about strength gained through loyalty and trust. It's about the value of compromise. It's funny, it's terrifying and it rings utterly true.

WAREHOUSE looks at a situation which, from the outside, seems utterly miserable and hopeless, but from the perspective of the players within the drama is extraordinarily rich in compassion, courage, and, strangely, optimism.

Keith Gray is an outstanding writer for teenagers. This is strong stuff, not in any gratuitously sensational way, but because it credits his readers with an understanding of life's big issues - trust, loyalty, courage and survival.

LINDSEY FRASER

For Baxter.
Why not?

KEITH GRAY

WAREHOUSE

RED FOX DEFiniTiONS

A RED FOX BOOK : 0099414252

First published in Great Britain by Red Fox
an imprint of Random House Children's Books

PRINTING HISTORY
A Red Fox paperback original 2002

3 5 7 9 10 8 6 4

Papers used by Random House Children's Books are natural, recyclable products made from
wood grown in sustainable forests. The manufacturing processes conform to the
environmental regulations of the country of origin.

Set in Adobe Garamond by Intype London Ltd
Red Fox Books are published by Random House Children's Books,
61-63 Uxbridge Road, London W5 5SA,
a division of The Random House Group Ltd,
in Australia by Random House Australia (Pty) Ltd,
20 Alfred Street, Milsons Point, Sydney, NSW 2061, Australia,
in New Zealand by Random House New Zealand Ltd,
18 Poland Road, Glenfield, Auckland 10, New Zealand,
and in South Africa by Random House (Pty) Ltd,
Endulini, 5A Jubilee Road, Parktown 2193, South Africa

THE RANDOM HOUSE GROUP Limited Reg. No. 954009
www.**kids**at**randomhouse**.co.uk

A CIP catalogue record for this book is available from the British Library.

Printed and bound in Great Britain by Bookmarque Ltd, Croydon, Surrey

THE TROUBLE WITH ROBBIE

Oᴎe

'I know a place you can go.'

Robbie was quick to his feet, brushing the rain and tears from his face with the back of his hand. He'd not even known the other lad was there until he'd spoken. There was a flash of embarrassment at being caught in this state, in the dark, in the gutter, but his distrust was stronger. He put a couple of extra steps between them.

The older kid stood in the lamppost's light. 'You look like crap.' Fact. There was no real sympathy. 'I can take you somewhere you can clean yourself up a bit.'

The rain cooled the patchwork of purple and blue running down the left side of Robbie's face, from his swollen-tight eye to his bloody lip. He touched his cheek self-consciously. His thin T-shirt was sodden, clinging to him. His ribs hurt like hell, with bruises all over the left side of his chest, but he was pleased the other kid couldn't tell.

'Seems stupid to be out here all night.'

He recognised the lad – school probably, but older than him. Maybe a friend of his brother's. Robbie took another step backwards, ready to turn and duck and run at the slightest sign.

'It's cool. No-one'll want to know anything. Everyone there's cool.'

The lad was lanky, stick-thin, kind of funny looking. His eyes and nose were squeezed up together in the middle of his face, but he had a huge mouth. His sandy-blond hair was darkened by the rain and plastered to his flat forehead.

Robbie kept his distance, but asked: 'Where . . .? Where is it?' He grimaced at the way his jaw hurt, making his words slur, making him sound drunk. He licked his busted lips. For a second there he thought he could taste his brother's knuckles. 'Is it far?' he managed.

'A bit. But there's a car round the corner we can use.' The boy's fleece jacket, two sizes too big and pricey by the look of it, was soaked and hanging shapelessly on him. 'I don't want this getting too wet.' He had a guitar in a black leather carry-case.

Robbie still didn't move as the older lad turned to lead the way. He watched him hurry off down the road, shoulders hunched against the rain. His suspicion was like pins and needles in his head, but he'd decided now that this lad wasn't a friend of his brother's. His brother liked his expensive shirts and trainers, his gold necklace and sovereign ring. This kid was too gawky looking. His brother would never have a friend like that. And it was this thought that made him follow.

The heat of the long summer's day was being washed away. The gutters were flooding, the streetlights illuminated solid sheets of the downpour, and the older lad hurried through them, running hunched up over the guitar. Robbie stayed those few paces behind. A late-night taxi bringing home a fare whooshed by, throwing up spray. They turned off the estate road into a short alley, backyard gates lining either side, several cars sitting in the rain. The older lad seemed to have it all planned, and strode up to an old blue Fiat.

'Hold this,' he told Robbie, giving him the guitar.

Fat droplets drummed on the car's tinny roof as he took a small hammer from inside his fleece. Then holding it between his knuckles, pulling his sleeve over to cover his fist, he smashed through the driver's side window with one quick punch. The sharp sound shocked Robbie, making him check up and down the shadowy alleyway nervously. But there was no-one around.

The older kid was sitting in the driver's seat in a matter of seconds, swapping the hammer for a screwdriver and snapping the steering lock, breaking open the flimsy black plastic of the steering column to get at the wires. The car farted into life, he pulled the choke out as far as it would go. It had taken him maybe half a minute.

'Get in. Just be careful with the guitar.' He was brushing away the shattered glass from under his backside.

Robbie was still looking up and down the alley. The little Fiat's engine sounded monstrous in the silence, but no-one came. He could feel his heart pounding.

'You coming?'

It was the older lad's face that made up his mind. He didn't look like someone who got arrested for nicking cars. The kid was a geek, a nerd, someone who girls laughed at and who got bullied on a regular basis. Someone like Robbie.

So he pushed the guitar over the seat into the back, and climbed in.

'Good choice,' the older kid said, and grinned like a letterbox.

As soon as Robbie slammed his door they were away. No lights until they were on the estate road. They turned left. Right would have taken them past Robbie's street, but he guessed he wasn't going home tonight.

'I'm Canner.' He was leaning forward in his seat, squinting out through the windscreen, the wipers doing the hard work. 'Or the Can Man. Whatever, I'm not fussed.' He wasn't rushing, just a steady forty.

Robbie was turning in his seat, looking out the back window, then to the sides, left and right. He was amazed there weren't police cars chasing them down. Where were the helicopters swooping overhead? Surely there should be spotlights, sirens, SWAT teams and '*Step away from the car with your hands above your head!*'

'That's what people call me.' He was rubbing his hair, shaking off the rain.

'What?' Robbie couldn't hide the nerves in his voice.

The older kid laughed, but not nastily. 'Don't look so worried. The police have probably got far better things to do than chase this old heap.'

'How do you know?'

'That's why I chose it. Only amateurs and those with a death-wish choose the decent cars. Maybe I'll go for a Saab or an Audi or something if I'm after the stereo, but I wouldn't even drive it out the front yard. People who swan around in big, chunky Saabs don't like them to go missing. But people who can only afford junk like this are often happy as Larry when the insurance money will buy them something newer. And, most important, they don't have alarms. My favourites are Jaguars. I love Jags; best cars in the world, ever. But I'm not stupid enough to nick one.'

Robbie's head was spinning too much to know if it sounded logical or not, but he was too wary of this kid to challenge him. He forced himself to face forward and shut up.

'I said that people call me Canner. Or the Can Man.'

Robbie nodded vacantly. He shivered with the wind rushing in through the broken window.

The older kid looked at him. 'So?' He raised his eyebrows. Then when Robbie still didn't answer, 'I know you're Frankie Hart's brother, but I'm guessing most people get to know you by your own name.'

Robbie was trying to work out where they were, but the gloomy, rain-slicked streets had become difficult to tell apart. They were in the town centre somewhere.

'Okay, then. Maybe they don't. Canner meet Frankie Hart's brother. Brother to Frankie Hart, meet the Can Man.'

Robbie turned to him, confused. 'What?'

Canner tutted and laughed again. 'No worries. Forget about it. If you want to play all shady and mysterious that's fine by me. Bit of cloak and dagger never did anyone any harm, I suppose.'

Robbie really wasn't listening to a single word Canner was saying. 'Where are we going?'

'A place I know.' He managed to catch Robbie's eye. 'Somewhere nobody's going to care about the state of your face.'

Robbie's fingers played along the bruising on his cheek. His eye was too tender to touch. 'I should go home.'

'Up to you,' Canner admitted. 'Say the word and I'll let you out here and now. But I'm guessing a bit of time away from whoever's got it in for you wouldn't be too bad an idea.'

Robbie frowned, biting on his lip, but didn't argue. He watched the way the wipers seemed to smear the red rear-lights of the car in front across the windscreen as they swept back and forth. His mum might be getting worried, he told himself. Might be. Might. He stayed quiet and let the older kid drive him because it was only *might*. Darkened shop windows slipped by.

They drove through the town centre, past the night clubs getting ready to kick out, the kebab shops getting ready to fill up. The Can Man seemed oblivious to any police cars they saw, and vice versa. They took the dual carriageway towards the industrial estate, then turned off just before they reached the docks.

Robbie had never been to the docks before, never needed to. Most of the dockyards were derelict, had been for the past twenty years or so. He knew that both his grandfathers had been trawlermen, but none of the kids at school came from fishing families now: the industry had all but dried up these days. They had a bright, new, sparkling clean shopping mall in the town centre instead. These days it was mothers who worked behind the counters in Boots or House of Fraser, rather than fathers who trawled out on the North Sea. Not that Robbie or the other kids his age had ever known any different. There was a Birds Eye fishfinger factory on the industrial estate, but it wasn't the same.

He might have heard MPs and councillors talking about 'renovating the dockland area' on the local news – not that he would have remembered. Government re-development grants meant nothing to him. And it appeared they meant little to the rest of the town as well, because the docks were still a mass of broken-down buildings, fallen businesses, blank windows, boarded-up doors, faded TO LET signs, rusting barbed-wire, vandalism and NO TRESPASSING – KEEP OUT notices.

The Can Man bumped the Fiat off the road onto a small patch of waste ground and pulled up behind a crumbling brick wall. Weeds and nettles reached up higher than the bonnet. He let the car stall itself by gently releasing the clutch, then reached behind him for the guitar. 'Just check the glove compartment for me, will you?'

Robbie did as he was asked. 'Just some tissues, and a George Michael *Greatest Hits* tape.'

The Can Man wasn't impressed. 'Typical middle-aged, middle-of-the-road cack. Better than Elton John, but worse than Sting. Leave it. If we take it with us some saddo's bound to want to play it, and I've had a rough enough day as it is.'

His chirpiness was almost catching. Robbie couldn't hide his nervousness and suspicion, but his face cracked briefly to allow for a small smile.

Canner climbed out of the car. 'Try not to tramp down too many weeds,' he said. 'Never know, it might still be here in the morning if I'm lucky.' He held the guitar high above his head and tiptoed his way through the nettles back onto the road. 'At least the rain's letting up.'

Robbie hadn't noticed, but Canner was right. The summer storm was passing, leaving a starry, cloudless sky and a slight chill to the air. He held his arm across his aching ribs and followed as the older lad led the way down narrow alleys, crossing silent roads, ducking through broken fences, jumping a tumbled wall. Everywhere was littered with rubbish; broken glass crunched beneath their trainers. The deeper they went between the forgotten and empty buildings the more Robbie began to realise just what kind of a situation he'd got himself into. Admittedly it was dark and everything looked the same, but even tomorrow in the glorious August sunshine this place would be a maze. He made sure he kept up.

'Hey, how old are you?' Canner called over his shoulder.

'Fifteen,' Robbie said, panting slightly.

'When're you sixteen?'

'November.'

The Can Man nodded. 'Okay, but do me a favour, yeah? If anyone asks, tell them you're already sixteen.'

'What for?' He knew he was particularly small for his age, and sometimes even had trouble getting people to believe he was fifteen.

Canner stopped and turned round to face him. 'You're going to meet a guy called Lem. He's one of the good guys. He's not the boss exactly, but what he says usually goes. He'll be okay if you're sixteen – you're legal to leave home, technically. He might be a bit funny if he knows you're only fifteen.'

'I'm not leaving home!'

'No, I'm not saying you are. Sixteen just means you're a missing person, but fifteen could mean you're a police file.' He grinned his letterbox grin. 'Less hassle if you're sixteen.' He hurried on, carrying the guitar in its black leather case like it was a baby.

Robbie hesitated. He'd never dreamed he could be leaving

home. He didn't have any money on him. How could you leave home without any money?

He began to wonder exactly where it was he was being taken. Stupid maybe, but his thoughts had been too full of getting caught stealing cars to really think about it until now. His first idea had been a shelter or a hostel or something – he'd seen them on the telly, run by charities for homeless people. Now he realised the Can Man had purposely left the stolen Fiat well away from where they were actually going, because wherever this place was, it was secret, hidden.

Still suspicious in his head, still nervous in his belly, he ran to catch up with the older lad because despite everything he couldn't curb a small feeling of excitement. Curiosity and rebellion moved within him. It was something he hardly ever felt, if at all. And it was a peculiarly *boyish* feeling. If he really was going to run away, he'd be doing it as much for the adventure as for any practical reasons.

They emerged from the narrow rat-runs and alleyways onto a wide rubble-strewn road. On the far side was water. Robbie could hear it more than actually see it in the darkness, slapping gently against the concrete walls of the disused quayside. Further along twin small cranes stood like giant letters from a mysterious alphabet, framed against the night sky. There were no boats. A cold breeze was carried off the water and he shivered in his sodden T-shirt.

On this side of the wide road stood a row of warehouses. Three-storey buildings of old brick with corrugated-iron roofs. Shuttered windows; they stared blank-faced across the man-made channel of slow water. Rusted padlocks that no key would ever be able to turn again sealed them up.

Robbie followed Canner along the road, dodging puddles and wreckage. It was awkward going. Half-bricks, lumps of concrete, chunks of metal and what seemed to be broken window frames with jagged shards of glass sticking up literally carpeted the deserted stretch of tarmac.

'It's our mess,' Canner explained. 'We did it. Makes it difficult for anyone in a car to get close.'

Robbie nodded. More secrecy.

'Oldest part of the docks, this,' Canner said, almost proudly.

He led the way into a cutting between two of the warehouses. There was a high slatted fence, but he knew which slat was loose and slipped through. There was a paint-spattered door in the warehouse on their right – no padlock, but a heavy bolt and a sign which read GUARD DOGS PATROLLING. 'A lie,' Canner said.

He slid the bolt back with a squawk of metal and heaved the door open, then stepped into the darkness of the warehouse and beckoned Robbie to follow. Robbie hesitated only slightly. Canner pulled the door closed and was able to draw the outside bolt back across by tugging on a loop of cable through a roughly cut slit on the inside. 'Nifty, eh?' he grinned.

Robbie nodded, but doubted the older lad could see him in the dim light. He looked around, trying to let his eyes get used to the dark. Not that they particularly needed to, because the place seemed empty. It was perhaps the size of a football pitch, with the old brick walls supported by huge wooden beams, almost as wide as he was. There was a faint smell to the air, damp, but not entirely unpleasant. Just to his left a steep set of stairs led up to a gantry-style walkway which ran around three of the four walls. He guessed it must lead to the floor above.

'Never use these stairs,' the Can Man warned him. 'They're not safe. On purpose.' He strode out into the darkness of the warehouse. Robbie, however, trod carefully. 'Don't worry about tripping up over anything. We try to keep the place obstacle free, 'cos we never allow any lights down here, obviously. And the rats'll avoid you.' He made sure Robbie was close behind him. 'It may be old, but it's safe as houses.'

Robbie didn't think houses were all that safe, actually. Wasn't his face proof of that?

He thought of his mum. She'd tried to stop him from running out tonight, claiming she'd talk to Frank, make him promise to leave Robbie alone. But she'd said it before. He'd heard it all before. And whatever she said only made Frank call him spineless anyway.

He realised he *wanted* her to be wondering where he was. He hoped she couldn't sleep for worry. He hoped she dragged his brother out of bed and forced him to go out looking for him. Because Frank certainly wouldn't be happy about it. Small revenge, maybe. But Robbie hoped it anyway.

There was a second set of stairs at the far wall. The Can Man bounded up them two at a time, still carrying the guitar in his arms. 'Sounds like there's a few up late,' he said.

Robbie could hear soft noises from the floor above. Muffled footsteps, faint voices. 'Are you sure this is going to be okay?' He didn't know what type of people to expect. He didn't even know what happened here.

'Don't see why not.'

'And this – this *Lem*? He won't mind?'

Canner shook his head without even looking back. 'So long as you stick to the rules.' He'd reached the top of the stairs and headed for a door a little further along the walkway, which creaked with every step.

'Rules?'

'Well – rule. Singular.' He turned back to face Robbie; walked right up to him and stared hard into his eyes, inspecting them, checking them out like a doctor. 'You into drugs?'

The question came as a shock. 'No! I never . . .'

He nodded approval. 'Didn't think you did.' Then carried

on along the walkway again. 'No drugs, that's the rule. Stick to it!'

'But . . .'

Canner disappeared through the door, and all Robbie could do was follow. Out of the main warehouse space, up three more dark stairs, then back again into the main building, but onto the first floor. And although he did it simply and easily – it was only a single step through an ordinary-looking doorway, after all – it somehow felt like stepping into a whole new world.

Two

It was a shanty town. But on the inside.

Robbie had seen shanty towns on the news, when the clean-suited but obviously sweaty BBC reporter was in Mexico or Africa or somewhere. Ramshackle huts and insubstantial lean-tos; haphazard and higgledy-piggledy and scruffy looking, all fighting for space. His first thoughts were of those kinds of places. But then he thought of music festivals too, like Glastonbury, because of the makeshift tents.

The people who lived here had built themselves whatever privacy they could. The obviously more industrious had managed to erect flimsy, wooden-walled rooms, but others had simply leaned doors against the side walls (or even against somebody else's room walls) to create personal dens. Shabby curtains hung from the roof beams to hide worn mattresses and sleeping bags. A couple of tepees were made out of roughly stitched bed sheets with the long supports nailed to the floor. There was even a little kid's Wendy house somebody had pinched from somewhere, looking very yellow, very bright in the dimness which surrounded it. A bare foot on a hairy ankle poked out through the door.

Robbie and Canner weaved their way towards the centre. It wasn't as dark as downstairs; there was an orange glow to see by. Robbie stared around, wide-eyed and more than a little apprehensive. He could hear muted music.

'We better find you somewhere you can get your head down,' Canner told him. 'Don't worry, there's always a couple of kips going free. Kinard will probably know better than me. I bet he's still up and about.'

'Are people asleep?' Robbie asked.

'Yeah, but don't worry about waking them. You learn to sleep like the dead in this place.'

At the centre of it all was an empty circle of space. Four grey portable heaters had been bunched together around their heavy blue gas bottles, but only one was burning – it was meant to be summer, after all. Three lads and a girl were sitting around on what looked like school chairs which were too small for them, smoking and chatting. The portable radio at their feet played subdued small-hours songs with the DJ whispering in between. A wooden box was being used as a makeshift table, with tin-can ashtrays and the melted smears of long-dead candles. They looked up as Canner and Robbie approached. It wasn't the heaters that were giving off the orange light, but the kind of free-standing warning lamps you see at roadworks. There were perhaps as many as fifteen or sixteen, fixed so they didn't flash.

'The usual suspects,' Canner said.

Robbie hung back a little, wondering which one was Lem, with his age restriction and his no-drugs rule.

The biggest of the three lads, the one in the baseball cap, nodded a greeting. 'Hey, Canner. Brought me something?'

The Can Man shook his head. ''Fraid not,' he said, holding the guitar to his chest. 'It's a special request for someone.'

The girl smiled. 'Hmm, I wonder if I can guess who that someone might be.' She waggled her eyebrows, one of which was pierced with a ring, making the others laugh. 'Pity she's already asleep. Now you'll have to wait until morning before you can do your knight-in-shining-armour bit.'

'I'm just doing her a favour, okay?' Canner protested. 'Same as I'd do for any of you lot.' The four of them jeered, and he turned to Robbie. 'One thing you'll quickly learn about this place,' he said, 'is that it's full of complete gits.'

Robbie must have looked shocked, because Canner had to smile before he realised it was a joke. He tried to laugh as well, but it was too late and it came out sounding forced.

Canner looked concerned. 'You all right?'

Robbie nodded quickly, but he was wondering if maybe he should have gone home after all. He took a deep breath and tried not to look too daunted or overwhelmed by everything. He was very conscious of his swollen eye, and couldn't help reaching up to touch his bruises again. He was waiting to see how long it would be before someone asked how he'd come by them.

'I'll introduce you.' Canner pointed at the biggest of the three lads, the one who'd spoken. 'That's Kinard.'

'Jeff,' he said. 'My real name's Jeff.' He was at least twenty, and massive like a heavyweight boxer. Dark-skinned and bull-necked, shoulders as wide as a truck. He was dressed in cargo pants and T-shirt. He re-arranged his baseball cap. 'I prefer Jeff.'

'But no-one calls him Jeff,' Canner explained. 'We call him *Kinard* because he's good at fighting.'

Everybody laughed again. Robbie just smiled, thinking it must be a private joke.

'Pete,' said the blond-haired lad in the England footie shirt. He didn't look much older than Robbie: his cheeks weren't as dark with stubble as the other twos'. He was sitting the closest, and clamping his cigarette between his lips he held out his hand to be shaken.

The third lad, with his long, greasy hair pulled into a ponytail, called himself Riley. Robbie was surprised to hear his American accent. 'Cigarette?' he asked. But Robbie shook his head.

'He's a new guy like you,' Canner said. 'Only been here a

few days, and how the hell he got here from whatever place in the sun he comes from, it scares me to think.'

Riley simply winked.

Canner turned to the girl. 'And this thorn in my side is Stef.'

She was the only one not smoking. She pulled a face at Canner, but lifted her hand in a quick wave for Robbie. She was wearing a baggy sleeveless top and he could see she didn't shave under her arms. He found the sight peculiarly off-putting, even shocking. It certainly wasn't something he'd seen on the glossy models in *FHM*.

'So what's your name?' she asked.

Robbie realised he was staring at her, but couldn't help it. She was maybe eighteen or so, and pretty too. Yet she had purple hair in rag-tailed dreadlocks, and piercings not only in her ears, but in her eyebrow, both nostrils and her bottom lip as well. To him it was as if she was purposely trying to make herself ugly.

'He's Clark,' Canner said, slapping Robbie on the back.

Stef smiled. 'Clark?'

'As in "Kent",' Canner explained. 'He's got a top-secret alter ego that he wants no-one to know about.'

Robbie was more confused than ever. 'I'm Robbie,' he said, bewildered.

'Ah-ha! So now you open up.' The Can Man threw an arm round his shoulder. 'I feel honoured. Thank you.' He grinned his letterbox grin.

'What d'you mean?' This was one of those awful one-step-behind feelings Robbie often had around older people he didn't know very well. His nerves made him shrug Canner's arm away, and his embarrassment flared purple beneath his bruises. 'What're you on about?' His body tensed instinctively, as ready as ever to turn and duck and run.

'Just a joke,' Canner said, taking a step back, trying to hold up his hands in a placatory gesture but finding it difficult because of the guitar. 'Don't mean to offend.'

'That's your problem,' Kinard told him, blowing smoke. 'You offend people too easily.' He took a drag on his cigarette. 'I reckon it's your face. I know *I* find it offensive.' The others laughed. 'Come on, give us a go on that guitar.'

Canner shook his head. 'As if! I'm not letting those gorilla shovels you call hands anywhere near this.'

Stef squinted slyly. 'You've got to keep it pure and un-sullied for the lovely lady, is that right?'

'I'm just doing her a *favour*,' Canner insisted.

'And hopefully she'll do you one back?' Riley smirked.

Canner tried to look outraged. 'Hey, there's no need . . .' But he simply didn't have the face for it.

'I've heard she's a bit of an ice maiden.'

Stef was grinning. 'If anyone can thaw her the Can Man can. How lucky must a girl be to hold the heartstrings of the great Can Man himself?'

As smoothly as that they'd stopped Robbie from feeling as though he was the centre of attention. No-one even seemed to notice he was there any more, so he let his nerves settle again.

He stayed quiet, and listened to them talk. They seemed like old friends, as if they'd known each other for years, and yet they never talked about themselves or each other. There was a certain distance kept between them. No-one was very far away from a sarcastic remark, and they all took it in turns to be the focus of some joke or other. Robbie liked that. It was the complete opposite of what he was used to. Especially with his brother, where a simple single clumsy word would undoubtedly end with Frank's raised fists.

The night's events were catching up on him. He was tired now and couldn't help yawning deeply. He was pleased when Riley announced, 'I'm shot. I'll see you guys in the morning,' and he was able to take his chair in front of the heater.

Canner watched the American walk away. 'He looks as though he's fitting in quick enough. What's he like?' he asked.

'Okay, I suppose,' Stef said. 'Why?'

Canner shook his head. 'Doesn't matter. Just seems a bit up himself at times. Like most Yanks, I suppose.'

Stef turned to Robbie. 'So what do you think of the Crap Palace, then?' she asked him.

Robbie frowned. 'The what?'

'This place,' Pete explained. 'We call it the Crap Palace.'

Robbie shrugged. 'Why?'

'Why what?'

'Why d'you call it the Crap Palace?'

'Well, it's not a very good one, is it?'

When they all laughed Robbie had to force a smile again, feeling like he'd been set up for yet another joke that he'd somehow missed.

Kinard turned to the Can Man. 'Come on. Trust me.' He held out his hands for the guitar. But Canner shied away.

Stef shook her head at him. 'My my, you've got it bad for her, haven't you?'

'I'm just doing her—'

'A favour,' Stef finished. 'Yeah, we know. But, come on. That must have been tricky to get hold of, even for you. Where'd you find a guitar at this time of night?'

'Let's just say there's a boring beardie-weirdie folk singer whose pub performance was cut short.'

Stef rolled her eyes.

'He had *two*. What's he need *two* for?'

'And all because the lady loves—'

'Can we change the subject?' Canner asked quickly. 'Look, Robbie here's just about done in.' Robbie nodded to prove he was. 'He needs a spare kip for the night. I'm guessing one of you must know one that's going.'

Pete nodded. 'Matty's is free. He left on Tuesday.'

Canner looked surprised. 'Yeah? I didn't know that. He gone back home, has he?'

'He was heading for Sheffield, he reckoned. Then maybe Manchester.'

Kinard said: 'He's got his head sorted. He'll be okay.'

Robbie's curiosity was sufficiently piqued to ask: 'How many people live here?'

Kinard blew smoke like a sigh. 'Depends. Some are only here a night or two, and then we never see them again. Don't even find out what they're called half the time. Most of us kind of come and go as we please. Lem's probably the only one you could say actually lives here.'

'Where's he sleep?' Robbie asked, looking around for the biggest and best-built room (or 'kip', as the others called them).

Kinard pointed up to the ceiling. 'He stays up top, likes to keep himself to himself.'

'There's more people upstairs?'

'Only Lem. Oh, and the Can Man here, of course.'

Canner shrugged. 'He trusts me.'

'What's he like?' Robbie asked, a little timidly. Already in his mind he'd pictured some kind of shadow man, restlessly pacing the dark, empty floor above. Never sleeping, ever watchful.

'He's about the best bloke you could ever want to meet,' Canner said. And nobody disagreed.

Robbie's curiosity spilled over. 'What's he do exactly? Why's he here?'

Nobody answered.

'I mean, has he run away from home? Are you running away, Kinard?'

Stef stood up quickly, suddenly ready to leave. Pete stubbed out his cigarette on the sole of his boot and then was also on his feet, keeping his head down.

Kinard turned to Robbie, speaking very flat and even. 'Have I asked you who decided to sharpen their knuckles on your face?'

Robbie recoiled from him instantly.

Kinard spoke calmly enough. 'I'm not being mean, kid, but you've got to understand: we don't ask, so you don't ask. Yeah?'

'Yeah,' Robbie said, nodding deliberately, scared all over again. 'Yeah. Sorry. I'm really sorry. I didn't mean . . .'

Kinard held up his huge hands. Peace. 'No worries as far as I'm concerned,' he said. 'You've just put the wind up these two, that's all.' He hooked a thumb at Stef and Pete. 'They must have *really* big secrets.'

They smiled, albeit awkwardly.

Canner stepped in. 'Matty's kip is the one next to that bald Geordie bloke's, isn't it?'

'The Geordie's tent collapsed,' Pete said. 'That's why he pinched that Wendy house from Toys "Я" Us.'

'It's him in there, is it? I should have recognised the snores. Come on,' he said to Robbie. 'You look knackered. I'll show you where you can get your head down.'

Robbie tried to apologise again, but both Pete and Kinard brushed it off with a wave of a hand. Pete was already lighting up again.

Stef said: 'Come find me in the morning and I'll get you some breakfast.'

'There's an offer you can't refuse,' Kinard told him.

Robbie nodded, half-smiled. He followed Canner through the kips to one of the makeshift tents. It was an A-frame of wood covered in thick, red velvet curtains, standing only about shoulder high, but longer than he was tall. It was just about wide enough to fit a single mattress inside. It looked suspiciously like a rabbit run.

Canner poked his head through the door flap. 'I think there's blankets and that in there,' he said. 'And Matty didn't have any tropical diseases that I know of, so you should be fine.'

Robbie nodded. 'Yeah,' he said quietly. Canner turned to go, but Robbie wouldn't let him. 'I really didn't mean—'

Canner put a hand on his shoulder. 'Hey, don't worry about it. The main thing is, you know now, yeah? People are here to get away from all sorts of stuff, and nine out of ten of them prefer not to talk about it. Why do you think I brought you here? So you could sort yourself out without having to answer awkward questions.'

'Thank you,' he said, and meant it.

'You heard what they said. People stay here as long as they feel like it. Just so long as they stick to the rule, they come and go as they please. That means you too now.'

'But it's a secret, right?'

'Sort of. But then again, not exactly. I'm not saying never tell anyone – it's just this place is usually found by those who need it most anyway.'

Robbie thought he understood.

'And if *you* ever need anything, come see me. Anything you want, okay?'

'Okay.'

'That's why they call me the Can Man. If you want it, I can get it.'

'Even guitars,' Robbie said.

Canner smiled widely. 'Exactly. You learn quick, after all. Even guitars.'

With that the sound of an off-key twang filled the air. Canner swore. He'd left it with the others. 'Kinard!' he shouted, not giving a damn for the people sleeping all around them. He ran back towards the others in the centre.

Robbie crawled slowly into his second-hand tent-type thing. It was pitch-black inside. He lay stiffly on his back on the lumpy mattress – he couldn't roll on his side because his ribs hurt too much. He could hear Canner and Kinard, Pete and Stef talking quietly. He listened for his name, and was relieved no-one mentioned him. The radio played an old song he recognised.

He didn't have a clue what time it was. He hadn't been thinking straight when he'd run out of the house earlier. He'd just wanted to be somewhere – anywhere – else, so he didn't have his watch. He just knew he was tired right through to his very bones. Even so it seemed to take an age to fall asleep. Too much stuff running around his head; it took him a while to slow everything down enough to be able to sleep.

But at least he was somewhere else now. At least he was out of his brother's reach for a little while.

'Crap Palace' – because it's not very good, is it?

And suddenly he got the joke.

So he laughed out loud, even though it was far too late. But it made him feel better all the same.

THREE

The warehouse – everyone who stayed there, everything that happened there – fascinated Robbie. It didn't take long for his mind to draw a solid line between what was happening to him now and what had happened 'outside'.

Waking on that first Saturday morning was admittedly an uphill struggle. His rumbling belly helped, as did the lumpy mattress. He opened his eyes to the close darkness of his borrowed kip and was aware of the faint smell of a stranger. But it wasn't either of these sensations that helped him remember the day before.

He felt like he'd been mown down by a juggernaut. His ribs squeezed painfully tight whenever he breathed too deeply, and his bruised face and jaw were one big nasty aching. He was frightened by how much it hurt. Every time his brother raised his fists he was scared that something inside would snap or shatter or burst and never repair. He'd been lucky so far (he gently hugged his arm against his sore ribs, testing the pain, and worked his tender jaw); hopefully he'd been lucky this time too. But things seemed to be getting worse, and Frank was getting angrier and angrier every time.

His mum would definitely be worried by now. Good, he thought. She'd be hassling Frank, crying and stuff, she could be a right drama queen. He didn't feel particularly big inside about making her cry, because he loved her, obviously. But she had a way of twisting things, a way of making whatever happened to anyone else seem to affect her worst of all. Even with him and Frank. Even when he was having seven shades knocked out of him she'd make it seem like she was the one hurting most. She'd start crying and her mascara would run and she'd lock herself in her bedroom, and all the time she'd be going on about their dad leaving her alone to cope with two violent sons. But the way Robbie saw it, she only had one violent son, because *he* never actually managed to do much hitting back, did he?

So if she started the drama stuff on Frank – good. Good good good.

He could hear a couple of different radios playing this morning. Crawling out of his borrowed kip he was surprised to see daylight streaming in through open shutters – surprised because his immediate thought was that it would surely be some kind of give-away to anyone outside. But as he'd learn over the next few days, nothing was done in the warehouse without consideration to how it might look from the outside; Lem saw to that. The thick shafts of sunlight didn't quite fill the space – one or two kips still hid in the dim corners – but it gave the surrounding confusion an unexpected touch of warmth. The place felt less dangerous; still chaotic and shabby but no longer intimidating.

And that feeling returned to him, the one he'd had last night following the Can Man through the rat-runs in the rain. That feeling of boyish adventure. He wanted to find Canner and Kinard and Stef. He wanted to know what people did here.

He noticed an apple just at the foot of his kip, a shiny green one. He was hungry, starving, but thought that it obviously had to be somebody's.

Stealing would be the quickest way to make enemies. He'd made enough mistakes last night, maybe made a bit of an idiot of himself too, and he wanted to fit in badly enough to leave the apple exactly where it was.

He'd expected bustle and chatter and laughter, but disappointingly there was hardly anyone around. He wandered between the kips. Some of them had graffiti scrawled across their doors. Looking closer he realised they were lists of names and dates:

Tilman 2/12–18/12
Kev 2/2–10/4 – spacious studio flat now available, apply within
Jess 12 April–6 June – God bless this kip and all who sleep in her
Brodie 7 July – until the day I die!!!

One had a hand-painted sign reading: 22 CRAP PALACE AVENUE. Another had a grubby welcome mat with 'UN' written on it.

He tried peeking inside some of the open doors or pulled-back curtains to see if anyone was there. He wanted to say, 'Hi, I'm in the gang too,' but the few people he did see either wouldn't meet his eye or scowled at him for intruding. He wondered where everybody else had gone, what they did during the day? Even the hairy ankle of the Geordie bloke had disappeared from the Wendy house.

'They're begging. Or stealing. Whatever.' It was Riley who told him, the American guy with the ponytail. He was sitting alone cross-legged in the centre, smoking, continually shuffling a pack of cards.

His answer shocked Robbie. He didn't think he wanted to have to do either of those things. He remembered all too well how panicky he'd been last night when the Can Man had stolen that Fiat. And begging? Well, *beggars* did that.

Riley didn't show any sign of having noticed the look on his face. 'How's your blackjack, Robbie?' he asked.

Robbie shrugged. 'Never played it, I don't think.'

'Never played blackjack?' He dealt him two cards. 'What've you got?'

'Er . . . King of Hearts, and Four of Spades.'

'That makes fourteen, okay? Picture cards count as ten. You've gotta make twenty-one without going over.'

Robbie clicked. 'Oh, right; pontoon.' One Christmas a few years ago (what seemed more like decades ago for some reason) his dad had taught him and Frank how to play. Back when things had been normal. For some reason the memory was a really strong one: the three of them, stuffed with turkey, giggling, shouting '*Twist!*' and '*Sssss-tick!*' and '*You're bust!*' at the tops of their voices. Their dad had been drinking his whisky – he received a bottle every year at Christmas. Robbie had got bored after a while, whereas Frank had stayed playing for hours. Their dad had even let him try some of his whisky, making Frank gag at the heat of it. But Frank had always been especially close to their dad, closer than Robbie.

Riley nodded, stubbing out his cigarette. 'Pontoon; okay. Whatever floats your boat.' He took a box of matches out of his pocket and spilled them by his feet, mixing them up with several weeks' worth of scattered dead ones which littered the floor. 'I'll make you a gambling man if it's the last thing I do.' He pushed roughly half of the matches towards Robbie. 'Dead ones are a dollar, live ones count as five. I want to win enough for my plane ticket home, Robbie –' he used one of the live matches to light a fresh cigarette – 'and this smoke's costing me four bucks, so let's get playing before I end up having to swim all the way.'

Robbie let him deal, played a couple of hands (which he lost), then asked: 'What do you mean, begging and stealing?'

Riley held his cigarette between his lips as he played, squinting through the smoke in his eyes. 'Maybe I should warn you: matches don't really buy plane tickets, my friend.' He laughed at Robbie's bafflement. 'Matches don't buy food neither. We need your very English pounds and pence to do that, don't we? Most of them beg for it, Robbie. Those who don't, maybe steal. What else is there?' He sighed, looked at his cards. 'So, what're you playing?'

Robbie checked his own cards, not really thinking about the game any more. 'Er . . . Twist.'

'"Twist".' Riley mimicked his accent. 'Come on! Get into it! Say "Hit me!"'

'Hit me,' Robbie tried tentatively.

Riley slapped a Jack down between them. 'And, bust! You're outta here. Maybe you shoulda kept to your twisting after all.'

Robbie shrugged his shoulders, as if it didn't matter. 'Do *you* steal stuff?' he asked quietly.

Riley watched him carefully through a breath of smoke. 'I steal,' he said.

Robbie nodded, pulling a face he hoped looked casual, trying to appear as though he knew loads of people who stole.

'Are you after something in particular? I've got a nice cell phone if you want it. Internet access. Can let you have it at a good price.'

Robbie shook his head. 'No. No, it's okay, thanks.'

'Well, anything you need, Robbie. You know where to come.'

'The Can Man said to go to *him* if I needed anything.'

Riley blew a long, long breath of smoke. 'Ah, yes. Good old Can Man. His heart of gold's gonna put me out of business.' He pulled hard on his cigarette.

A heavy, thickset lad with short, spiky dreadlocks joined them. Riley immediately grabbed up his cards and announced: 'Poker!' He divided the matches into three piles and introduced Jan.

Jan nodded 'Hi' to Robbie, and hunkered down with them on the wooden floor. He was wearing a combat-green muscle

T-shirt and at the top of his wide right arm was an elaborate dragon tattoo. Robbie thought it looked fantastic, the dark ink against Jan's dark skin.

'You good at poker?' Jan asked him.

Robbie tried to make a joke. 'I played strip poker once when I was at junior school.' He blushed when nobody laughed.

Jan frowned at Riley. 'What kind of dirty boys you getting me involved with?' Turning to Robbie again he said: 'You keep *all* your clothes on when I'm around, you hear?'

Riley dealt the cards. 'I'll teach you boys to play the Vegas way.'

They played for what seemed like hours, Robbie and Jan fairly quiet, Riley being vocal enough for the three of them. Robbie really got into it, even though he wasn't much good. It felt kind of adult to be playing poker, like cowboys in a saloon bar. He'd never been particularly brilliant at complicated games, and he kept getting confused between the hands, which was better than which – straight, flush, two pair. It was almost as difficult to get the hang of as chess, and he was rubbish at that. He watched his pile of matches dwindle while Riley's pile grew – he was an expert bluffer.

Others arrived and drifted in and out of the game. At one point they had eight players and at least ten people watching them.

Pete in the England shirt from last night joined in only to lose worse than Robbie. He complained about it loudly, claiming Riley was cheating. Riley sighed deeply and stood up to face him. 'I might get insulted if you're not careful, my friend.' Pete met his eye for a second, then stalked angrily away. Riley simply smiled. 'Another one bites the dust, eh, Robbie?'

Robbie nodded and smiled back, but didn't look up from his cards. He hadn't really noticed what had happened: he had two pair to worry about. And he hadn't been the only one – everybody else had been staring just as intently at their cards too.

The problem was that the winnings became worth less and less because most of the players smoked, and soon there were only a few live matches left. But Robbie was having one of the best times ever. He'd already told Jan that he was going to get a dragon tattoo exactly the same as his (Jan replied he'd only need to get an 'iddy-biddy baby one' unless he grew some proper muscles). He hadn't exactly forgotten his grumbling stomach or his aching ribs, but he wouldn't move because he didn't want to miss out on being a part of what was happening.

He wasn't sure how old Riley was, or Jan, or any of the others. Sixteen? Seventeen? Twenty? Most were older than him for sure, but they were still letting him play, that was the point. At school you didn't hang around with anyone who wasn't your own age; each year stuck pretty much to themselves. It was uncool to be seen with kids younger than you, and you in turn weren't cool enough to be seen with anyone older. But here, nobody seemed to care who you were.

He won a hand: full house, queens and tens – complete fluke, but a brilliant hand. Riley clapped him on the back, then asked if he could borrow the one and only live match amongst the winnings. And Robbie gave it to him happily. He grinned when three others crowded around the single flame. He was thinking that maybe it was worth begging and stealing to stay here.

He couldn't help feeling disappointed when the game eventually broke up and people began to drift away.

'Hi.' It was Stef. 'How's it going?'

Robbie beamed at her; he was like a little kid at Christmas. 'Yeah, great. Fantastic. This place is wicked. Everybody's wicked.'

Stef didn't look too sure. She just nodded very slightly, then said: 'I don't mean to sound funny, but you maybe ought to clean yourself up a bit.' She gestured in an apologetic kind of way at his face. 'You've still got some blood around your nose.'

Robbie simply hadn't been aware of how close he'd come to forgetting about what had happened yesterday, on the outside. He was suddenly embarrassed by the state of his face and stared at the floor so she couldn't see him properly. 'Is there a toilet?' he asked, also realising how badly he needed to go.

'There's a couple downstairs. They're kind of manky, but you get used to hovering. Just be grateful they flush.' She pulled her face into a half-grimace. 'The best thing to do is head outside,' she told him. 'There's a couple of McDonald's, a Burger King and KFC all within walking distance, and if you time it right you can get washed in their toilets without anybody bothering. Just keep swapping between the four of them and no-one remembers your face.'

Robbie knew well enough where they were, but didn't know how to get out of the docks themselves. No way could he remember all the alleyways Canner had used yesterday. 'I'll be okay downstairs,' he said.

Stef was about to leave him to it, but asked: 'Hey – did you get your breakfast?'

Robbie shook his head. His stomach rumbled as if on cue.

'I left you an apple outside your kip. I promised you breakfast, remember?'

He suddenly brightened. 'Yeah, I saw it. Thanks. I forgot.' He was so hungry his mouth watered as he pictured that big shiny green apple. 'I thought it was somebody else's. I'll get it now. Thanks, Stef. Thanks.' He hurried between the kips back to his curtain-tent.

But the big shiny green apple had gone. His heart sank and his stomach groaned. Somebody had taken it.

Stef had followed him, probably knowing full well that the apple wouldn't be there any more. 'Somebody's pinched it,' she said.

'Maybe they've just put it inside for me,' Robbie tried hopefully.

'Come on,' Stef said. 'I've got some more at my kip.'

Robbie checked under the loose flaps of the curtains anyway, not really wanting it to be true that someone had stolen it. Then he had to follow Stef, his hands as empty as his belly.

Her kip was against the far wall and was one of the better-built wooden rooms, although it still looked like a person-sized hutch to Robbie. The low door was chicken mesh stretched across a frame, with a pale blanket covering. She kept it padlocked. Like most kips there was no ceiling/roof, but the walls were tall enough to give a good feeling of privacy. He was surprised by how much room there was, enough for maybe two double mattresses side by side. Stef, however, only had a single one pushed up against the warehouse wall. She had a locked suitcase as a headboard. There was a white blouse and a black skirt hanging neatly on a peg on one wall. She lit a couple of candles. Thumbprint-smeared photos of people having fun were Blu-tacked all around.

'Did you build this?' Robbie asked. He'd noticed there was no list of names on the outside.

Stef nodded as she pulled out the suitcase and unlocked it. 'Me and my boyfriend.'

'Oh yeah? Have I met him?' He was thinking it could be somebody he'd played cards with, and was searching the photos for a face he recognised. 'What's his name?'

'His name is *scum*. And no, you've not met him. He's long gone – let's hope he stays that way.'

Robbie dropped his eyes from the photos and sat down. He'd learned last night when to stay quiet.

Among the few clothes in her suitcase Stef had a bag of five delicious-looking apples, and she handed one to Robbie. He took it gratefully, thanking her, then devoured it in five bites. He didn't refuse when she offered him a second. His stomach murmured its gratitude, forgiving him, and he managed to vocalise this with a small belch.

He watched her as she ate her own apple. He wondered if she fancied him. Because why else would she have invited him into her kip? Why else would she be giving him apples? He looked her up and down, asking himself whether or not he could fancy her back. But her clothes were baggy and he couldn't tell what kind of breasts she had. And her armpits and all of the stuff in her face put him off. He'd never had a girlfriend before, but he'd always imagined that when he did she'd wear tight tops and shave under her arms. Like girls should. He began to wonder if there was a girl like that living in the warehouse.

'What's up?' She'd caught him staring.

He blushed. 'Nothing. Nothing, honest. Just, you know . . . These apples are dead nice. Thanks.'

'Do you want another?'

'Yeah. Yeah, thanks.' He stuffed the third one away just as quickly, and suddenly wondered how she'd got the apples in the first place. 'Stef . . .' He wiped the juice from his chin. 'I know I'm not supposed to ask questions . . .'

'Who told you that?'

'Well, last night when I asked Kinard why he—'

'Wrong question, that's all. Some questions are okay.'

He nodded. 'Oh, right. Okay, then.'

She was staring at him now. 'Go on, then.'

'What?'

'Ask me a question.' She sat up straight in expectation, pulling a serious face.

He fidgeted, looking at the apple and not her. 'Do you beg and steal?'

'*I* don't, no. But I know most of the people in here do.' She gestured at the white blouse and black skirt. 'I work in a pub. The Breech on Danes Street? The landlord's okay about paying me cash-in-hand. There's a couple of others who work places too. Why?'

'Will I have to beg and steal if I want to stay here?'

Stef was shocked. 'What?'

'I think it's fantastic here, and I want to stay as long as I can. It's just . . .'

'Jesus, Robbie! No-one *wants* to stay here.' She shook her head, angry at him. 'People don't come here for fun, you know. People come here because they're screwed up, and this is all they've got. You don't come here for a holiday! You come here because you've got nowhere else to go. And because your life's a million times worse on the outside.'

Then she suddenly stopped, her anger draining with the realisation. She hung her head. 'Oh God. I'm sorry. Look, I'm really sorry, Robbie.'

He was touching his swollen eye, the bruising on his cheek.

'Canner wouldn't have brought you if you didn't need . . .' She sighed deeply, and wrapped her arms around herself in a tight hug. 'This place isn't fantastic, Robbie. Not everybody here's fantastic.' She shrugged. 'Some arsehole stole your apple, right? And yeah, okay, it's only an apple, right? But it was all you had to eat, but they didn't care. And that's what this place is like.' She seemed desperate for him to understand. 'You can have a bit of fun playing cards for matches, but I've seen fights, bad fights, when they've been playing for money. People are only friendly here when they want to be, and that's not all that often really. If it wasn't for Lem kicking people out every now and again this place would be full of the worst scum in the universe. It's no place for a kid like you.'

'I'm not a kid.'

'How old are you, Robbie?'

'Sixteen,' he said, remembering what Canner had told him to say, but not able to meet her eye.

'Well, I reckon the Can Man's trained you well,' she said, seeing right through him. 'I reckon you're about fourteen or fifteen, and you only look about twelve. Although saying that, you're certainly not the youngest Canner's ever brought along. Not by a long shot. That's the problem with him and his best pal Lem, they've got it into their heads that they're on some kind of mission. Kinard's been getting just as bad too.'

Robbie felt like he was being told off by a teacher or something. He squirmed, plucking at the hem of his T-shirt.

And to be fair to Stef, she wasn't enjoying the role she was playing here.

'All I'm saying . . .' She sighed again, finding her words tough to come by. 'All I'm trying to say is, please don't aim to stay here. That's not the point. As soon as I raise enough money, I'm gone, I'm away. You won't see me for dust. You should do the same. As soon as whatever's messed up on the outside is sorted, you should go.'

Robbie got to his feet. Deep down a part of him guessed what she was saying was probably true. But she was making him feel like a little kid again, making him feel dumb again.

'Thanks for the apples,' he said. 'I'll pay you back as soon as I can.' He was surprised to see how upset Stef looked. More than sad. She was close to tears. And that made him want to get away even quicker.

'I don't want paying back,' she said. And threw him the last apple.

'I will, though,' he told her. 'I will.' He ducked out as soon as he saw the first tear roll down her cheek.

Four

'You in there, Robbie? Hey! Come on.'

He'd been kind of hoping whoever it was would just give up and go away.

'Robbie!'

But no such luck. So he crawled shakily from his kip to see Kinard and another lad waiting for him. Kinard put a heavy hand on his shoulder. 'Fancy a trip outside?'

Robbie shrugged. He squeezed his eyes shut and shook his head to try and rattle some sense into himself – he hadn't a clue what time it was, having slept for most of the day. It felt dark enough to be night outside, and the warehouse was lit by the orange glow of the roadwork lights.

'Won't take long,' the second lad said.

Robbie didn't recognise him. He could have been as old as Kinard; dark spiky hair, wearing a long, tatty leather coat, faded black T-shirt and jeans. He was unusually pale, and his face was badly marked by acne scars. The way he stood made him seem particularly sure of himself. To Robbie he looked like he could handle himself in a fight, even though he was nowhere near as heavy brick-built as Kinard.

'Come on,' Kinard said, a hand on Robbie's back, steering him between the kips towards the stairs without giving him time to object.

Robbie had the idea to just keep quiet. It suddenly occurred to him that he might be getting kicked out. Maybe Lem didn't want him in his Crap Palace any more and had sent his henchmen to do the dirty work. He ran through the past two days in his head, trying to think what he'd done wrong.

He'd spent the rest of Saturday avoiding Stef, that was for sure. He couldn't understand what was wrong with her. He'd thought she was weird anyway, what with the way she dressed and that, but why she'd suddenly started crying was a mystery to him, Bermuda Triangle stuff. To be honest, it had freaked him out a bit. So instead of getting involved, he'd simply stayed clear. Not that it had been too difficult because she hadn't been hanging around the centre much anyway. He reckoned she was probably working in that pub.

Then again, he might not have remembered even if she had been there yesterday. He'd been out of it from pretty early on.

Someone had appeared with two cases of cheap red wine, Bulgarian or something, and had willingly shared it around. Three or four bottles were opened at once – the corks pushed down into the necks because no-one had a corkscrew – and when they came round the circle to Robbie he took big, hearty gulps. He knew they'd been stolen, and he knew how concerned he'd been about stealing, but . . . The bottles passed round the circle, and every time one came to him he'd smiled and knocked it back. He'd never drunk alcohol before – even at Christmas dinner his parents had always refused him – and after two days of eating so very little he was soon feeling the effects.

It tasted worse coming back up. On the way down it was vinegary enough, but it seared his throat and nose on its return journey. The warehouse had rocked and swayed like it was stuck up a tree on a windy day, but everybody had found it funny and had kept offering him more and more. He'd laughed right along with them. At the puke down his front. At the way soft chunks of pre-chewed apple shot out his nose. Real funny. Until he'd woken up this morning.

He'd felt as bad as he did when Frank had a go at him. Worse even.

So he'd spent much of today crouched over one of the disgusting toilets downstairs, heaving his stomach raw. But it was worth it, right? Because they'd let him be part of the gang. They'd let him drink with them, they'd thought he was funny. At school even the teachers found it tough remembering his name. Stef was so wrong, he'd told himself, as his stomach had kicked and only acid and stringy phlegm had come up. She just didn't understand. He'd do this as often as it took as long as he made friends.

But now . . .

He followed Kinard out into the warm night air, onto the abandoned quayside, and wondered if he'd said something to someone when he was drunk, or done something wrong. Maybe he'd started asking questions again.

They headed down an alleyway in between the warehouses, and came out onto a parallel road where Canner was waiting for them, sitting in the driver's seat of the old blue Fiat he'd stolen the other night. Robbie was surprised to see he had a black eye.

'Take your time, why don't you?' Canner said, trying to hide the bruising by turning his face away. The car's engine was already running.

'Robbie's fault,' Kinard said. 'Took him a while to drag himself out of his kip.'

Canner looked Robbie up and down. 'I heard about last night. God! Look at the state of you!'

Robbie desperately tried to read his face. Was he being serious? Or was there a hint of mickey-taking in his expression? He was shocked the Can Man was here at all. And hurt. Surely Canner wouldn't be trying to kick Robbie out, not when he'd been the one to bring him here in the first place.

Kinard somehow managed to squeeze himself into the

front seat, the poor car groaning with his weight. The third lad held the back door open for Robbie, but Robbie didn't move.

'Come on. Hurry up,' Canner told him. But when Robbie still didn't move he asked: 'What's up?'

'Where are you taking me?'

Canner glanced at the other two; everybody looked awkward. He asked Robbie: 'Have they not told you?'

Kinard shrugged.

'I thought you'd seen him this afternoon,' the third lad said.

'I did,' Canner admitted. 'But he was dead to the world, so I didn't feel like waking him.'

'Are you kicking me out?'

The three of them turned to look at him. 'Why?' Canner asked. 'What've you done?' A sly grin slid across his face. 'Got a guilty conscience, have you?'

The lad dressed in black tutted. 'Shut up, Canner.' He walked round to the boot of the car and opened it up, gesturing for Robbie to follow him. The small boot was packed full of roadwork lights. 'The batteries in these are dead; we just need to get some more. I asked Canner to get you to give us a hand. But you don't have to if you don't want to.'

Relief made Robbie smile. 'No, it's all right. I don't mind.'

'Okay, then.' The older lad slammed the boot shut. 'So let's get going.'

Robbie nodded quickly. 'Yeah.'

Canner drove them out of the docks and onto the dual carriageway: he was heading out of town. He talked away about the day's events on the outside – some of what had happened to him, a bit of what was going on in the rest of the world. He sounded like a lively, gossiping newsreader. Kinard and the other lad asked the occasional question –

when they got the chance, when Canner paused for breath – but Robbie was too relieved he wasn't getting kicked out to join in at first. He sat in the back with the lad in black and watched the town slip by. He might only have been inside the warehouse for a grand total of nearly three days, but it felt like he'd somehow forgotten a lot of what he was now seeing actually existed.

'Hey, Robbie!' Canner shouted over his shoulder. 'Don't take this personally, but you stink! When was the last time you had a wash? It's like a dog died in here, even with this smashed window.'

Robbie was too shocked and embarrassed to reply.

'I mean, Je-sus! Did you sleep in that T-shirt last night? Crusty puke and all? Crusty Bulgarian puke, which isn't the best, trust me.'

Kinard lashed out quickly, punching him in the arm, making him yelp and swerve the car. 'Give the kid a break,' he growled.

'Give him a break?! Give him some mouthwash more like it. That death-breath of his is melting the back of my head!'

'As delicate as ever, eh, Canner?' the lad sitting next to Robbie said. 'Crap Palace and its guests have never been the most fragrant of people.'

'Yeah, I know, but—'

Kinard cut him off. 'Did your new woman like her guitar?'

'Like it? She loved it!' Canner beamed. 'And I mean *loved* it!'

Kinard smiled too. 'Did she thank you?'

'Yeah. Of course.' Canner's letterbox grin was literally from ear to ear.

'And just *how* did she thank you?' Kinard asked. 'Giving someone a black eye is a strange way of expressing gratitude where I come from.'

Canner blushed and reached up quickly to touch his

bruises in a way Robbie recognised all too well. For once the Can Man was quiet.

Robbie was grateful to Kinard, but now he couldn't help being especially conscious of the filthiness of his T-shirt, the greasiness of his hair. He rolled down his window and tried to breathe out of it, pretending he was just enjoying the night air.

He realised they weren't driving away from the town, but around it, skirting its edges, keeping away from the centre's busy roads. They were actually getting pretty close to where he lived, to where the Can Man had found him – not that he said so.

When they pulled over opposite his school's main gates, no more than a ten-minute walk from his house, he couldn't help feeling suspicious again. Very suspicious. However, at the far end of the street was the four-way junction the Council were widening to make into a mini-roundabout and pelican crossing. Teachers and parents were always complaining about how dangerous the crossroads were. And now that something was at last being done to solve the problem, everybody was moaning about the havoc caused by the temporary traffic lights at either end of the school day. But all around the junction, flashing away, was a whole host of warning lights exactly the same as the ones in the boot.

Robbie gave the gloomy school building a hateful glare. They'd moved three times in the past four years since his dad had left, and this was the worst school by a long shot. The holidays couldn't come quick enough for him – he'd been desperate to get away. And now he wondered if he could escape the place for ever by staying in the warehouse.

Canner was talking to him. 'You listening, Robbie?'

'What? Sorry.'

'You will be if we get caught,' Kinard told him.

Canner turned round in his seat. 'I hated that place too,' he said, nodding at the school.

Robbie followed his gaze back through the high gates, remembering that he'd recognised Canner as someone in his brother's year.

'The teachers were okay, I suppose. I was never much good at maths, and Mr Rider was always picking on me, but it was nobheads like your brother who made me really loathe being there.'

Robbie met his eyes, and a brief acknowledgement, a quick signal of understanding, passed between them. He looked back at the school. He'd hardly been there the last few months, preferring to wander the streets waiting for home time instead.

'But anyway,' Canner continued, 'what I was saying was, the idea is to swap the dead lights in the boot for some fresh ones, okay?' Robbie nodded, looking up the street. 'The workmen'll just think the batteries have run out quicker than expected. Hopefully no-one should know anything's been nicked, swapped, messed with, whatever. Clever, eh?' Robbie nodded again. Canner turned back to face the front again, putting the Fiat into gear. 'So I'll keep the engine running while you three do the business. If I think we've been spotted I'll rev the engine twice – honking the horn only draws more attention. I know how nosy people are round here, so we've got to be quick and quiet.'

They drove slowly up to the junction, crossed it, and Canner pulled up with the car facing away from the road-works. There was no other traffic. 'Quick, then,' he said.

Kinard, Robbie and the lad in black jumped out. Kinard was at the boot, Robbie was picking up the closest lights. He couldn't help glancing at the houses, at the front windows with lights on behind the curtains, waiting for one to twitch. But there was nothing to worry about. It did strike him that they didn't really need four people to do this, but maybe being asked to help out was a compliment, so he wasn't about to question the logic. He collected the fresh lights and gave them to Kinard, who switched them off to save their batteries, while the other lad put out the dead ones. Simple, quick and easy.

Or at least it should have been. They managed to squeeze an extra couple into the boot, Kinard slammed it closed with a thump, and the Fiat's engine died.

The big lad held up his hands. 'Wasn't me!'

They heard Canner swear and rushed round to the driver's side to see what the problem was. He was scratching the bare wires together to get a spark and pumping the pedal, but the little car could only whine and cough. It wouldn't start again.

Canner pounded on the steering wheel. 'I think we've run out of petrol,' he said, sounding as if he didn't quite believe it.

'How the hell did you let that happen?' Kinard asked.

'Hey, here's an idea: blame me, why don't you!' All Canner could do was point at the fuel gauge which still read three-quarters full. 'I don't get it.' But when he slapped the dial the needle dropped instantly towards empty. 'Crappy foreign piece of crap!' he shouted, grabbing the steering wheel and trying to shake it loose.

'Maybe if you hadn't been using it to take women out on the town . . .'

Canner glared at him.

'Don't panic, it's not a problem.' The third lad leaned calmly past Kinard and opened the door, beckoning Canner out. 'You can get us another one?'

'Of course I can!' Canner sounded offended by the question.

'So, what're you waiting for?'

'Something half-decent for a start.' He climbed out. 'You,' he said to the car, wagging a finger. '*You* are gonna be recycled as a tin of beans. And I don't mean Heinz – oh no. I'm talking Kwik Save "No Frills" for you.'

'Yeah, like it's really scared,' Kinard sneered.

'And you can sod off too!' Canner snarled.

The lad put his finger to his lips. Shush. 'So let's just remember we're breaking too many laws to mention at the moment, yeah? And let's try not to get caught for any of them.'

Canner stalked away towards a line of cars a little further up the street, but couldn't resist a quick kick of the Fiat's front wheel as he went. 'God give me a Ford,' he muttered under his breath, taking his small hammer from his pocket.

Robbie had watched it all in an odd state of bemusement, which turned to laughter as the Can Man stomped away, mumbling to himself.

'Best not to,' the lad in black told him with a wink. 'You'll only encourage him.' His voice was light, but he was checking the surrounding houses for peering faces. 'Let's get the lights back out, ready for him when he finds something.'

Which in hindsight was a mistake. They had the boot of the Fiat open, a cluster of lights at their feet, Kinard holding one in each hand, when the full beams of the police car swung round the corner and picked them out like actors on the stage.

FIVE

'Walk away,' the lad in black hissed. 'Just walk. Slowly.'

Kinard put the lights down on the road and turned his back on the police car. He walked calmly, steadily down the middle of the road. Robbie followed the way he went but kept to the pavement. The lad in black was at his shoulder. Robbie was looking up the street trying to spot Canner, dreading the sound of smashing glass, but he couldn't see him in the shadows between the cars.

'The Can Man's good at looking after himself,' the other lad said, as if reading Robbie's mind.

The police car drew very slowly, almost crawled its way, alongside Kinard. The two coppers inside were both watching him. 'What're you up to, son?' the one in the passenger seat asked.

'Just walking.' Kinard didn't look at them.

The car pulled forward to stop a little way in front of him. The copper was opening his door. 'Are you and your friends going to tell us what you were doing with those lights?' He was stepping out.

Kinard turned to Robbie and the other lad, pulled a face like he was saying sorry, then suddenly took off at full sprint up the street. The copper was out of the car and in pursuit, but Kinard had a good head start.

The lad in black grabbed Robbie's arm. 'This way!' They ran in the opposite direction.

They were across the junction and to the school. The older lad boosted Robbie up and over the railings, and was quick to follow: a check over their shoulders to see the police car turning in the street to come after them. They ran in between the dark buildings, past the science labs, down the steps next to the library. Their feet echoed loudly on the concrete path. Robbie struggled to keep up. After a day of losing everything in his stomach he had no energy to keep him going.

On to the playing fields, but Robbie's companion was heading the wrong way.

'You can't get out that way,' Robbie shouted. 'There's a gap in the fence over here.' The other lad followed him across the football pitch.

They crawled on their bellies underneath the fence into somebody's back garden, clambered awkwardly through high bushes into next door and crouched behind a greenhouse, as much out of sight as possible. Then, and only then, did the older lad let them stop to catch their breath. He pulled his long leather coat around himself. Robbie's lungs were on fire. He was shaking with the exertion, his whole body trembling, sweaty. His heart hammered away.

'You okay?'

Robbie nodded, sucking in the biggest lungfuls of air he could, as silently as he could. He leaned against the smeared glass of the greenhouse. 'Do you think they followed us into the school?'

'Didn't look like it, but I reckon it's probably best not to hang around too long. Lucky for us you knew about that gap under the fence.'

Robbie nodded again. He didn't admit that the only reason he knew about it was because a gang of kids had found it funny one dinner time to shove him under and block it up, trapping him, while they shouted, 'Oi! Oi, mister! There's someone in your garden, mister!'

'Do you know where we are?' the older lad whispered. 'Because I haven't got a clue.'

Robbie thought about it, trying to picture the pattern of streets around the school in his head. 'Garland Road, I think.'

'How far are we from the coppers?'

'Not far enough,' Robbie said, not meaning it to be a joke, but the older lad laughed all the same. 'Will Canner and Kinard be okay?'

'Kinard will be fine, he's been in worse situations. And the Can Man is very probably enjoying himself. It's us we need to worry about.' He looked around, back the way they'd come. 'Pity we landed in a row of terraces. There would have been nothing simpler than casually strolling down the driveway and back onto the street.'

'They're all terraces round here,' Robbie told him.

'I don't fancy going back into the school, do you?' Robbie shook his head. 'Looks like we're in for some garden-creeping. Ever been creeping?' Again Robbie shook his head. 'It's the best fun you can have on dark nights,' the older lad told him with a wink. 'The Can Man's an expert.'

He poked his head round the side of the greenhouse, obviously checking the house for any signs of life. Then he waited – waited for what seemed like a long time to Robbie. At last he whispered: 'Stay close,' and dashed for the wooden fence opposite, his long coat like a cloak behind him.

It was a quick scramble up and over into next door. They were able to stay well away from the houses because the gardens were narrow but long. The lad in black was only a step ahead of Robbie, leaping the flowerbeds, sprinting across the patchy lawn to the next fence, head down all the way. Across this garden, through the tatty hedge, and into the next. They ducked through the frame of a child's swing, and jumped the scattered toys. They struggled over the wall. No toys in this garden, but no bushes to hide behind either. They sprinted across the grass as fast as they could.

This fence was high. Robbie's companion stopped to help him over, boosting him up. Robbie grabbed the top and only saw the dog as he got ready to swing himself over. He tried to stop his body's forward motion, but he was still being pushed from behind. He tipped and rolled, then fell, landing painfully and buckling his ankle. The dog was quick to bark. It was only a scruffy mongrel but it was loud, and it had teeth. It planted its front legs and lowered its head, snapping and snarling.

Robbie froze. He was dead. The older lad would be crazy to follow him.

But he did. He swung himself down from the fence and without a second's hesitation leapt at the dog screaming, waving his arms like a lunatic.

'Yaaaah, you ugly buggaaaaahhh!'

The dog turned tail and ran from him, its bark more like a yelp. Robbie almost laughed out loud, but lights came on in the windows and he was hot on the heels of the older lad. The dog kept barking from a safe distance. They got to the next fence as the back door opened, but they were too quick. Up and over into next-door, behind a shed, between the bushes, one more fence and at last to the end of the terraced row.

They ran down the alleyway and out onto the street. They didn't stop running until they turned the corner at the far end. The older lad's face was shiny with sweat, but he was grinning from ear to ear. 'That brought back memories,' he said.

Robbie's chest hurt with the lack of breath. 'How come . . .? How did you know that dog wouldn't go for you?' he managed to ask.

'I didn't,' was the reply. Then: 'Come on, let's keep moving, okay?'

They crossed between the parked cars. There were no

police around, but the lad in black looked uncomfortable somehow, now that they were back out in the open. 'What we need is a phone,' he said. 'Canner's got a mobile we can call him on to come and pick us up. Do you know where there's a phone box around here?' He felt in his jeans pockets, and swore. 'More importantly, I don't suppose you've got any change on you?'

Robbie shook his head.

His companion bit his lip and frowned. He looked jumpy. 'I don't like the idea of being stuck quite so far away from the warehouse.' He turned up and down the street, as if looking for an answer. 'Damn!'

Robbie was surprised by how agitated the older lad had suddenly become. It made him feel all the more nervous too. Maybe it was because he was all dressed in black, but it made him think of a vampire caught in the open just before the sun was about to rise.

'We better get moving anyway,' the older lad said, clearly not happy with what was happening. 'I don't think it's the brightest idea going back to the car – even Canner's not cracked enough to do that – so let's just head for home. Which way?' Then when Robbie pointed, 'Sorry, Robbie, this is my fault. I knew something like this could happen.'

'How were you supposed to know the police would show up?'

'I've got a confession,' he said. 'I told Canner to bring you along because I wanted to talk to you. All my idea, I'm afraid. And it's gone a bit pear-shaped.'

'Why did you want to talk to me? What about?'

'Just stuff,' he said. 'Being nosy, I suppose. Interested to know who the new guy was.' Then: 'Come on. The sooner we're back at the warehouse the better for everyone.' But he turned to head off in the wrong direction.

Robbie grabbed his arm. 'No, it's this way.'

The lad swore again. 'Not used to being out and about,' he admitted, shaking his head at himself. 'And certainly not this far from the warehouse.' He sighed heavily. 'Kind of pathetic, I know. If only we could call Canner.'

Robbie knew of a phone they could use, though he wasn't sure if he was willing to say so at first. They weren't far from his house, but he didn't want to have to face his mum, and certainly not his brother.

They walked quickly, not talking at all, just keeping an eye out for the police (and hopefully either Canner or Kinard). The streets were mostly deserted, and every time they heard the sound of a car they didn't know whether to duck and hide or try to flag it down. It was when they passed the old man walking his dog that Robbie was forced to make up his mind. The man had noticed the state of his T-shirt, the filthy red stains all down the front, and had pulled a face as he hurried over to the other side of the road. Robbie realised that walking all the way across town looking like he did was bound to draw attention, might even get people asking questions, so he admitted to the other lad that his house was close by.

'We can phone Canner,' he said. 'And I can get a clean T-shirt or something. It's just . . .' Even as he spoke he knew that the anxiety was printed on his face as plain as day.

'Just you'd really rather not have to go there.'

Robbie shrugged, nodded, shrugged again. 'My brother might be there,' he said eventually. 'He . . .' His fingers moved to the bruising around his eye, but didn't quite touch it.

'I can see what he did.'

And suddenly some of the bile inside Robbie spilled out. 'It's ever since our dad left us. I think Frank blames me, you know, for him leaving. And then he gets drunk . . .' He forced himself to stop. If he didn't everything would come gushing out, tears and all, and he refused to cry here, now.

The older lad had a hand on his shoulder. 'Nobody's going

to force you to go back, certainly not me. That's the good thing about the warehouse, it's the somewhere else you can go when there's nowhere else left. And you can stay as long as you need to.'

'Unless Lem kicks me out.'

'Why would I want to kick you out?'

Robbie's mouth hung open. Which must have looked comical, because Lem laughed.

'Come on,' he said. 'I'm not exactly a big fan of the outside world, I kind of prefer what comforts Crap Palace has to offer. You can tell me all the nasty things the Can Man's been saying about me on the way. It's a long walk, so I'm hoping he's been saying plenty.'

But Robbie hung back. Now more than ever he wanted to use the phone at home. He told himself it was because he needed clean clothes, money, his watch. He told himself it was to help Lem out, and get them back to the warehouse quicker. Lem had saved him from that dog back there, so now he was simply returning the favour. And it *was* for all these reasons. But most of all he wanted to impress the older lad with his courage.

'It'll be okay,' he said, maybe to Lem, maybe to himself. 'We'll call Canner. It'll be okay.' Frank might even be out, but he doubted it.

Their house was in the middle of the terraced row. There were no gardens: the front doors opened straight onto the street. Robbie didn't like it, especially lying in bed late at night when he felt too close to the street's noise. Theirs was the green front door, the colour being its only distinguishing feature from the rest of the street.

His key was in his back pocket. Stepping into the hall he was embarrassed by the untidiness, which was silly really, when you considered where he was choosing to live now. But he'd always hated the muddy bikes with punctured tyres leaning against the stairs, the browny-yellow fag burns on the windowsills, the greasy wallpaper. The smell of stale cooking hung in the air. The carpet had a black damp patch underneath the radiator. The living-room door had a large crack running just off-centre from top to bottom. He wanted to tell Lem that they had lived in nice houses, not always ones like this, but he didn't know how to.

'Welcome to Crap House,' he whispered. 'Because it's not a very good one, is it?'

Lem smiled. 'Are you sure you're okay about this?'

Robbie nodded, but felt far from okay. There was no TV shouting in the living room, so he knew his mum must be out. She cleaned the estate agent's on Monday nights, which meant she usually finished early and managed time for a drink before she came home. He guessed she must have stayed for last orders. However, he could hear his brother's stereo coming from upstairs.

He had a sickly dread in his stomach. He pointed Lem towards the phone in the kitchen, then crept upstairs, hoping to grab what he needed and be gone again before anyone even noticed he'd been here. But when he got to the top of the stairs he could see his brother's bedroom door wide open, and suddenly Frank was there, glaring at him, accusing and furious.

'Where the hell have you been?' He was wearing a baggy white T-shirt with his thick gold chain on show at the neck. He was short, stocky, solid, with his dark hair cropped flat to his skull. He was a cannonball, always eager to destroy.

Robbie could have run, wanted to run, but pushed past him to his own bedroom. He slammed the door behind him.

Frank kicked it open. 'Have you been with Dad?'

The question surprised Robbie, confused him. Is that what his brother thought? His schoolbag was at the bottom of his wardrobe, buried under a mound of clothes, some of them clean. He grabbed what clean ones he could, stuffing them in the bag. Did Frank believe he'd gone to find their father?

'Where've you been? Where's Dad?'

'How should I know where he is?' He moved round the side of the bed, trying to keep it between him and his brother. But Frank stayed at his shoulder.

'Mum's going spare because of you. She's had the police round and everything. I'm talking to you! Where've you been?'

Robbie was doing his best to keep his back to his brother. He was looking for his watch, couldn't think where he'd left it, couldn't think straight with Frank shouting at him. Inside his top drawer was a shoebox he kept his measly savings in, and he scooped out the two fivers and the few coins that were left. He knew there should have been more, but Frank had probably stolen most of it. His watch was on the floor under a magazine. He stooped down for it.

'Don't ignore me!'

Frank's punch came out of nowhere, hitting hard and fast into Robbie's side, a rocket of hot pain exploding in his kidneys, doubling him up. He spilled the money from his hand, his knees folding beneath him, dropping him to the floor.

'I said, where've you been?'

Robbie looked up at his brother, dark and hateful, fists clenched, from where he was curled on the floor and realised this was how he would always remember him. He didn't need photographs in a family album. This view of his brother would never be forgotten. Sharp tears needled at the back of his eyes.

'Look at the state of you. I'm sick and tired of Mum running after you all the time. It makes me sick the way she babies you. And see the way you treat her!'

Robbie cast around on the floor, sweeping up the money that was close by, and reached for his bag. He knew that if his mother wasn't here, hovering over the phone, waiting for news, fretting, then she was doing all of her worrying down at the club with a vodka and orange. He had to use the end of his bed to get to his knees, not all that confident of being able to stand.

'I'm talking to you!' Frank stamped down on Robbie's trailing hand, the one clutching the money on the floor.

And something gave – Robbie felt it. The crack of his fingers was loud, like a shot. Something broke. He bucked and twisted away like an eel, screaming. He curled into a ball around his pain, sucking his breath through his sobs, cradling his fingers. The pain was too much, too much. He thought he was going to explode with it because he just couldn't keep it all in. He'd lost his fight against the tears now. Snot and tears ran in rivers.

'You're not going anywhere,' Frank told him.

'Leave him alone.' Lem stood in the bedroom doorway.

Frank rounded on him, raising his fists, not seeming to care who this intruder was or what the hell he was doing in his house.

Lem met his eyes. He took a black-handled knife out of his back pocket, opened its blade. 'Touch him one more time, just once, and I'll fuck you up.'

Frank didn't move. He didn't step forward, but nor did he lower his fists. His eyes flicked to the knife, to Lem, back to the knife. They settled on Lem, defiant, but steadier.

Robbie could read the nervy tension on Lem's strained face: it said quite clearly that this was the last situation he wanted to be getting himself involved in. And Robbie was worried his brother would see it too. But Frank still didn't move. This wasn't what usually happened. Okay, their mother was often wailing away in the background some-where, but she had always been easy to ignore. The bully didn't usually get bullied himself. Robbie could read the look on his brother's face too. This kid was taller than him, it was saying, but could he still take him?

Time froze for Robbie, the seconds stopped. Did he really want Frank to get cut up? Yes, of course he did. See what Frank had done to him. But did he? Did he really? He didn't know. He just wanted to get out. He just wanted to be somewhere else, because he couldn't be here. He got to his feet.

'Get out of my house!' Frank spat.

'I'm Robbie's friend. I'll leave when he does. Come on, Robbie. The Can Man's on his way.'

Frank laughed through his nose. 'Is this the kind of friend you've got now, Robbie? You hanging out with soap-dodgers, eh? Wait till I tell Mum.' There was a childish, needling edge to his voice.

Robbie somehow managed to get himself together, managed to gather up his money and his bag. His fingers were on fire. He was trying to wipe away the snot and tears. He held his hand up against his chest, nursing it. He thought the pain was going to make him puke.

'You're dead.' Frank was squaring up to Lem. 'I don't care who you are. I'm not gonna worry about it when I meet you on your own without your knife one night.'

Robbie pushed out of his bedroom and down the stairs. Lem followed him slowly, keeping between him and his brother.

'You watch for me, Soap-dodger. I'm gonna be looking for you.'

Back out on the street, Frank followed them all the way. Lem kept his eyes on his every move, the knife held down but ready. Robbie prayed for Canner to hurry up, because he knew it wouldn't take long for his brother to pluck up the courage to have a go.

'Drop the knife and see what you get,' Frank spat.

Lem simply smiled, but there were wires of tension in his face and jaw.

A car turned the corner and sped up the street towards them, a blue Ford Sierra. Robbie saw Canner and Kinard staring around, looking for them. They nearly shot right past, but he literally stepped out in front of them from between the parked cars, forcing Canner to stand hard on the brakes.

'Jesus!' he shouted from the driver's seat. 'Don't do that! I could've hit you. I didn't—' Then he spotted Robbie's tears, the way he held his hand. 'What . . .?' He saw Lem and Frank. He almost kicked the door open in his hurry to get out.

'It's okay, Canner,' Lem told him calmly. 'No worries here.'

'You okay, Robbie?' Canner asked doubtfully.

Robbie nodded. He just wanted to go. He just wanted to get away.

Frank recognised the Can Man and snorted derisive laughter. 'Should've known you're the one chumming up with my little brother! Always knew you were a queer-boy or something. I'll get you as well, you know. I'll get all three of you.'

Kinard climbed out of the passenger seat and came round the front of the car. 'You gonna get me too?' He flexed his shoulders, lifting his head high, holding his arms away from his sides slightly. He seemed to eclipse the whole street.

Frank stood his ground, but he shut up. His eyes glowed with fury, his face bloated with hate.

Robbie got into the car. Slowly, slow enough to make their point that they had all the time in the world because Frank didn't worry them one little bit, his three friends followed.

Frank shouted at him from the doorstep, 'And I'll get you, Robbie. You're not my brother no more. You don't know where my dad is. He wouldn't be hanging around with soap-dodgers and queer-boys. Wait till you're on your own, I'll get you.'

They drove away without looking back.

Six

Robbie was perched on the edge of Stef's mattress. She lit the candles, then sat down beside him. He winced when she took his hand, but more out of anticipation of the pain. Her fingers were slim and smooth and cool.

'It was my brother . . .'

'You don't have to tell me what happened.' She turned his hand over in hers. 'Your middle and third fingers are definitely broken. The others are just swollen. Why didn't they take you to a hospital?'

By 'they' she meant Canner, Kinnard and Lem, who'd all agreed Stef could do something to help Robbie and had rushed him to see her. But then she'd flatly refused to let the others into her kip. She'd even planted a firm hand on Canner's chest and asked him: 'Haven't you done enough for one night?' He'd tried to protest, but she'd closed her door on him.

'I don't want to go to the hospital,' Robbie said. 'I don't have to, do I?'

'I admit it's not going to kill you. But the best I can do is try to splint them somehow.'

Robbie nodded quickly. 'Anything.' Hospital would mean strangers asking questions, and he didn't want that. He felt like he needed to talk, but he didn't want the questions that were bound to follow. He just wanted to tell his side of it, all of it, then let it go and be done with it.

Stef dragged her suitcase out from the end of her mattress, and inside, underneath her neatly folded clothes, was what looked like a small lunch-box. Inside this, however, were some toiletries with a small roll of bandage and a packet of headache tablets. She popped a couple of the tablets from the foil and gave them to Robbie. 'Should help with the pain,' she said. She had to use a short pencil as a splint and bound his broken fingers together. 'Every day in this place I feel more and more like somebody's mum,' she told him with a hollow laugh.

Robbie watched her as she kept the bandage in place with one hand and plucked a safety-pin from the waistband of her skirt with the other. She used it to carefully secure his bandage. 'Guess I'll have to put on a bit of weight to fill it out again,' she said, running her fingers around the now baggy skirt. 'Not many times you'll hear a girl say that.'

He smiled with her, and there was a rush of gratitude inside him, like a can of Coke fizzing over when it's been shaken up too much.

'I'm sorry I've been avoiding you,' he said.

She raised a single eyebrow, the one with the piercing. 'Have you? I didn't realise.' She kept her eyes on what she was doing. 'Maybe I should have kept my mouth shut anyway. It's not as though you deserved a lecture, is it?'

All Robbie could do was shrug.

Someone knocked quietly on the side of the kip. Stef shouted: 'If that's the Can Man he can—'

But it was Lem who poked his head in through the door. He glanced at Stef nervously. 'I just wanted to make sure Robbie's okay.'

Stef tutted at him, but didn't stop him from coming inside. He squatted down on his haunches, watching her as she carefully pinned the bandage.

'Does that feel too tight?' she asked.

Robbie shook his head.

'How're you doing?' Lem asked him.

'Okay,' he said quietly.

Stef packed her things back into her suitcase. She looked up at Lem from under a disapproving frown. 'Are you here to apologise to him? I'm guessing you had something to do with it.'

Lem looked almost apologetic. 'Give me a break, Stef, will you? How was I supposed to know that—'

'How long will it be before they get better?' Robbie tried to flex his fingers but the pain was too great.

'A long time, probably,' Stef told him.

'Sometimes nothing seems to get any better.'

'You can say that again,' Lem admitted.

'*I* want to get better, though.'

Stef and Lem were quiet. As ever, there was a radio playing somewhere in the warehouse.

Robbie knew you weren't supposed to talk about things in here; he knew most people kept things locked up inside, but . . . 'Frank never used to be like this. Just when my dad left us, I think he blamed me.'

Before their father ran out on them, Frank had never bullied Robbie. They'd had the usual brotherly squabbles and cat-fights obviously, with their mother screaming at them to stop their bickering because it was driving her up the wall, but nothing like the spitefulness which had gone on for the past four years. Only once before their dad left had Robbie received such a vicious beating from his brother. It was when he was eight, and Frank was eleven, maybe twelve. He told Stef and Lem what had happened.

'I'd been playing this game, and it was all an accident really, but I told this lie and everything seemed to go really weird. And it was like watching a film, with everything happening all around me that I couldn't stop and make better.'

He used to play a lot by himself when he was younger, always inventing games that he acted out alone. This particular day wasn't too long after Christmas, it was still the holidays, but Robbie had been playing in the grounds of his primary school. He knew he shouldn't have been there; it was just that the school was the perfect setting for the game he'd just made up: Kidnappers.

His imaginary friends had been kidnapped, and they'd been tied up in different places around the school – maybe in the classrooms, maybe in the sports hall – and only Robbie could rescue them. He had to be careful, though, because the place was booby-trapped with trip wires, landmines and laser cannons. He sneaked around the buildings, the perfect action hero, tough and daring.

He made all the noises himself: the helicopter flying him into the danger zone, the laser cannons firing, the voices of the characters. He made the sound of the landmine exploding when he accidentally stepped on it. But the sound itself wasn't exciting enough. It needed more excitement, to match the enjoyment of the rest of the game.

It was a cold day, one of those days when you could see your breath. Robbie was wrapped up in his bobble hat, gloves and scarf, and he had the idea of throwing these in the air as he leapt off the ground, tumbling over and making the loudest exploding *boom* he could. It would look fantastic, like part of *him* was exploding.

So he did just that. *Boom*! He flung his gloves and hat and scarf to scatter like debris, and it looked fantastic, just like a real explosion. But in his enthusiasm he'd thrown his hat so hard it had sailed away to land on the roof of Miss Harper's classroom. He knew he had to get it back – it was a Christmas present and his mum would go mad if he went home without it.

He was able to climb onto the bike-shed roof first. The sheets of thin corrugated metal buckled and wobbled beneath him, but from there he could easily get onto Miss Harper's roof. He was quick; there was no-one around; he grabbed his bobble hat and hurried to get down. But the rusty old roof of the bike shed really wasn't safe, nowhere near strong enough for people to run on.

He heard a crack and felt it go from under him; he couldn't save himself. With a snapping, crunching sound the whole thing collapsed. He crashed down amidst the flimsy sheets of metal, smacking his back and banging his legs on the solid struts of the bike stands below. He thought he was going to die it hurt so much. He'd winded himself and had to fight for his breath. He was very lucky to be able walk away from such a fall, but despite the pain he managed to stand, and on unsteady, shaky legs scurried away in case anybody came to see what all the noise had been. He ran all the way home clutching his bobble hat.

He went to bed early, and of course never told a soul what he'd done. He suffered silently with the bruising on his back and legs, always making sure they were covered up when his mum and dad were around.

When he went back to school the following week the bike shed's collapsed roof had been removed completely, and everybody complained about their bikes getting rained on. They had a special assembly in which Mr Patrick condemned vandals and the damage they did. He said that if anybody knew who had been responsible for wrecking the bike shed they should speak to him in his office. Of course nobody did, because Robbie had been on his own, and he thought he'd got away with it.

It was when he was getting changed for PE that everything started going wrong. Jordan Green saw the huge blue and purple bruises covering his back like a strange map, and started shouting other people to come and look. Miss Harper also wanted to see, and she wanted to know how Robbie had got such terrible injuries.

He didn't know what to say. He couldn't tell the truth so he kept saying he'd fallen over, he'd just fallen over. He'd fallen off his bike, he said. Then he said he'd fallen out of a tree. Miss Harper took him to see Mr Patrick, who asked if his parents had seen them. Which was when Robbie told the lie. It suddenly sprang into his head. He'd heard that girl with curly blonde hair in the other class say it, and everybody had been nice to her, so he said it too.

'My dad did it.'

And everything changed. Everything went wrong.

It was all kind of blurry in Robbie's memory now, but there had been police and social workers, and people had said nasty things about his dad. But Robbie hadn't been able to tell the truth: the lie had grown a life of its own. There had been so much trouble.

His dad had looked pale, with dark shadows under his eyes. He'd been angry and confused. He'd looked at Robbie strangely, sadly, had kept asking him why he'd said such a bad thing. He'd never laid a finger on either of the brothers, didn't even spank them, but nobody seemed to believe him. Robbie remembered it as a horrible, angry, scary time.

Things had only settled down when Robbie had finally admitted the truth. There had been more shouting, more arguments, although not as bad, nowhere near as bad. They still had visits from a social worker, but over the weeks things slowly got better. His dad looked better, started speaking to him more. All Robbie wanted was to be forgiven.

It was Frank who told him that their dad had nearly ended up in jail. Robbie didn't know whether to believe him or not. Frank said that if the police had taken their dad away it would have all been Robbie's fault, and had cried at the thought of losing their dad. It had shocked Robbie to see his big brother burst into tears like that, so shocking he'd burst into tears too.

That was the first time Frank beat him up.

'Frank had always been really close to Dad,' Robbie said.

Stef had listened without saying a word. She was staring at her hands. 'Robbie, I—'

But Lem was angry. 'Don't you dare try telling me you deserve what your brother's done! You were only eight. Trust me, we all do stupid things, even at eighteen.' He pointed at Robbie's roughly bound fingers. 'But no way should you go round thinking you deserve that.'

'But you don't understand how close Frank was to him,' Robbie said. 'He never let my dad alone. He always wanted to be like him. That's why he drinks whisky now, I think. Because that's what Dad's favourite drink was.'

Lem sighed – not bored, just at a loss. 'Who knows why your dad ran out on you? You said he didn't go until you were eleven, and that's three years after whatever you did.'

'But I think Frank still blames me.'

'Or maybe he blames himself, and just takes it out on you. Or maybe he blames your mum but knows he can't hit her, so takes it out on you. Or maybe he's just a vicious, spiteful, screwed-up thug. You'd have to be a psychologist to figure it all out. The thing that matters is you don't have to worry about him any more. When – if – you ever feel like going home, fine. See your mum, put her mind at ease. But for now, use this place.'

Robbie simply nodded. He plucked at his bandage.

'You know, you could go to the police if you wanted to,' Stef said.

Both Robbie and Lem looked at her, shocked.

She turned to meet Lem's eyes. 'Most people would probably say you should've gone to them straight away.' And Lem had to look away first.

The thing that surprised Robbie was that he'd never even considered going to the police. It wasn't because he was trying to protect his brother; it was just that the police were simply more adults, like teachers and social workers and his mum. Nobody like that had helped in the past. So he shook his head. He wanted to stay in the warehouse.

'Nobody here would stop you if you wanted to get the police involved,' Lem said slowly. 'I'd make sure of that.'

'I know,' Robbie said.

'It's your choice,' Stef told him.

Robbie shook his head. 'I'm okay.'

Lem stood up, stretched his legs; his knees popped. 'Listen, the real reason I wanted to see you was because I reckon I owe you a thank-you.'

Robbie frowned now, not sure what he meant.

'You went back to your house for me. So I could call Canner. So I could get back here as soon as possible. It was a brave thing to do, and I just wanted to say thanks.' He smiled slightly. 'So, you know, thanks.'

Robbie smiled with him, then said: 'I can stay here as long as I want, can't I?'

'No worries. You know how this place works.'

That was all Robbie wanted. He stood up to leave.

Stef said: 'Robbie, I'm really sorry about what's happened and . . .'

But he shook his head. 'It doesn't matter. Honest. I just wanted to tell someone, you know?' He turned to Lem. 'I just wanted somebody to know.'

It was true: he wasn't looking for someone to comfort him, or to give him false promises of how everything would be better in the long run. With any luck, he'd be able to sort things out for himself.

'Thank you for bandaging my fingers,' he said, and ducked out through the doorway.

Seven

Pete, with his England shirt, had claimed he needed to get to a town with a decent team now that the football season was about to start, and before he left that afternoon he'd let Robbie take over his shabby kip. It was a not quite square room made of rows of old doors nailed together, with a couple of sagging sheets to give it some kind of roof. It looked as though it might all come crashing down if you sneezed too hard. Robbie had got some candles off Kinard to light the inside, but had become scared that the sheet roof might catch fire, so he'd borrowed two of the roadwork lamps instead and the inside was lit up orange.

'Robbie? You in there?' Kinard never knocked, only shouted. He came inside and when he stood upright the top of his head pushed at the sheets. So he sat down and lit a cigarette. 'How's your fingers?'

'Still hurting,' Robbie admitted.

'You ought to get Canner to get you some more painkillers.'

'Yeah, I will. But they're not as bad as this morning.' He'd slept on them last night without realising and had woken up in agony.

'That's good, then.' Kinard blew smoke decisively. 'What about the rest of you?'

'I'm fine.'

'Yeah?'

'Think so.'

Kinard puffed at his cigarette. 'D'you still want showing around the docks?'

'Yeah. Yeah, definitely.' Robbie nodded quickly. He was still worried about wandering around and getting lost. He didn't want to leave the warehouse and never be able to find his way back.

'Come on, then.' Kinard rose up to his full height again, literally head and shoulders above anything Robbie could ever hope to reach. 'Now's as good a time as any.'

Robbie was on his feet to follow, but at that moment Canner suddenly shoved his head in through the door. 'Kinard, I think Lem might need you,' he said, looking serious. 'Someone's carrying.'

Kinard swore, and was immediately pushing out of the door, past Canner. 'Who?' He pushed so hard the whole kip swayed.

'That American, Riley. I *knew* there was something about him.'

'Where are they?'

'Lem's going to Riley's kip. And Riley doesn't know we know.'

Robbie followed them out of the kip. It was the rule. And if someone was carrying, then it had been broken.

Canner led the way over to the far side of the warehouse. Others must have heard the rumours because they followed on. Robbie could feel the tension in the air. He saw Lem bang on the side of Riley's kip – definitely one of the better-built rooms, nearly twice the size of most people's – and realised that most of the tension seemed to be coming from him. He looked paler than ever.

Lem saw Robbie and Canner and Kinard, and quickly shook his head at Kinard, letting him know to stay back for now. 'Riley.' He slapped the flat of his hand against the wood. 'Riley!'

The American opened the door like he was welcoming guests to a dinner party. He scanned the faces crowded around, winked at Robbie, smiled widely at Canner and finally settled on Lem. 'Problem?'

'Maybe,' Lem admitted. 'Are you carrying?'

Riley squinted at him, his eyes narrowing. 'Somebody say I am?' He scanned the faces again, this time holding his gaze level on the Can Man.

'I want to check your kip,' Lem said, stepping forward.

Riley held up his hands to block him. 'Whoa there, Lemmy Boy! Private property, you know?'

'If there's nothing to be found, you've got nothing to worry about.'

Riley took his time lighting a cigarette. 'What makes you think I'm just gonna let you search through my stuff? *My* stuff, you see?'

'If I'm wrong then I'll apologise and even buy you a drink to prove no hard feelings.' The words were friendly, but everyone standing there knew that the tone of Lem's voice was far from happy. There was real anger in him, and he seemed to be having trouble holding it back.

'No hard feelings . . .' Riley pondered.

'Everyone knows the rule,' Canner piped up.

'"Everyone knows the rule."' Riley mimicked Canner's English accent. 'Well, rule schmule,' he told him, laying the American on thick and heavy. He looked back at Lem. '*Your* rule, by the way. Who made *you* king of the castle?'

Lem stared hard at the American, his eyes boring into him. It seemed to take a lot of effort for him to tear his gaze away. He turned to look at the faces around them. He found Robbie's. 'Him,' he said. 'He made me king. And so did he.' He pointed at Canner. 'And him, and her – him too. All these people standing here, all these people under this roof. They made me king.'

Riley squinted through the smoke from his cigarette. He still had a gleam of fire and spite in his eyes, but he stepped aside.

Lem motioned for Canner, and the sandy-haired lad ducked inside. There was a complete hush apart from the sound of the Can Man rummaging around through bags and boxes. Everybody else was quiet, hardly daring to breathe. Lem and the American stood like gunslingers. More people gathered; Stef was here. To Robbie it looked as if everybody had come to see what was happening. Kinard was being swallowed by the crowd and pushed through to the front, but Lem gave him a quick shake of the head and he retreated a few steps back again.

'Y'all don't make a mess in there, now,' Riley called in his whiny American accent.

Canner came out of the kip carrying a clear plastic bag about the size of an envelope. He nodded at Lem and held it up to show the pills inside. They looked like sweets to Robbie.

The American laughed drily, shaking his head.

'You're not welcome here,' Lem told him.

'You've gotta be kidding me! They're not mine, Lemmy Boy. How should I know whose they are?'

'You're not welcome,' Lem repeated, stepping forward. 'I don't want you here; they don't want you here. Get out!' Robbie thought he was going to take his knife out again, but Lem made no such movement. He didn't need to. Robbie realised this was the second time in only a few days he'd seen Lem facing somebody down, but this time was different. This time he was on home ground, and the confidence showed in the way he stood, the way he spoke.

Riley was shaking his head in disgust, blowing smoke. 'I don't believe this. I'm not letting you kick me onto the streets. Come on, here! I'm telling you those aren't mine.'

Again Kinard came forward, backing Lem up, and Canner joined them.

Riley held up his hands, submitting. 'Jesus Christ! You guys oughta take a look at yourselves. The Mafia's gonna be running scared because of you.' There was the ever-mocking edge to his voice, refusing to be humiliated. 'Just let me get my stuff.'

Lem was ready to step aside, but the Can Man was shaking his head. Lem questioned his friend with a look, but was willing to trust him. 'Just go. Now.'

'I've got expensive stuff in there,' the American whined.

'Forfeit,' Canner said.

Riley glared hatefully at him. 'You'll get yours,' he threatened.

'Don't want it if you've already had it,' Canner told him with his grin stretched extra wide.

Riley had lost – there was no way he could fight everyone. And Robbie was a little surprised that it was *everyone*. There was a shared feeling in the air. Robbie didn't know the posh word for it; he could only think of it as a team spirit, every-one together. The American had broken the rule, so he was out, no questions asked. No-one wanted him here. He had to back down. He made sure everyone could see his sneer as he tramped his cigarette into the floor, and then let Canner and Kinard usher him downstairs.

Robbie felt the tension go out of the crowd, listened as everybody began to breathe again. Talk broke out quickly: most of them had never seen something like this happen before; one or two remembered the last time it had.

Robbie moved over to Lem. 'I thought he was all right,' he said, not hiding the fact that he was a little unsettled by what he'd just witnessed. 'When we played poker he seemed all right to me.'

'The Can Man's call,' Lem said, the only one not to let the

tension go. His hands were still fists and he stood as if rooted to the spot.

'But what's he going to do if you're not letting him have any of his stuff?'

'Canner must know something we don't.' It took real effort for him to turn and walk away. 'It's not my problem now.'

EIGHT

Two days passed. Jan with his dragon tattoo followed Riley; everybody believed they were in things together. On the Thursday Canner turned up with a timid, anxious-looking girl called Lucy, and Robbie let her have his new kip. He was happy enough sleeping in his small makeshift tent, because sleeping was all he used it for. He'd spent the evenings chatting with Kinard in the centre, sitting like old men in their favourite armchairs. But he'd also spent a lot of time out and about, enjoying the last of the summer sun. Kinard had been as good as his word and had shown him every back alley and rat-run he knew. And then the Can Man had found him a job.

'Can you find me a job?' Robbie had asked.

'Of *course* I can,' had been the sharp reply, offended that there'd been doubt in Robbie's voice.

It was no great shakes admittedly: all he did was hand out leaflets on the high street, advertising restaurants or night clubs or clothes sales. Each morning at ten he met an old guy called George outside Argos who gave him a paperboy's bag full of leaflets. George always wore the same jumper no matter how sunny it was and reeked of BO. Robbie didn't know if he was too idle to hand out the leaflets himself and gave Robbie a cut for doing it, or whether he was the boss of the leaflet distribution business. Either way, it wasn't important. He picked a spot at the entrance to Safeway or Iceland and handed the leaflets to the shoppers as they hurried by, picking up any that were chucked on the ground by those who couldn't be bothered to walk as far as the bin themselves. He returned what was left to George when the shops closed at six, and received a tenner for his time. So the wage was peanuts, but it wasn't as if he had rent to pay. Stef had told him you could survive pretty cheaply on fruit and stuff; it was Big Macs and Kentucky Hot Wings that were expensive. And the weird thing was, he felt healthier for it.

He'd phoned his mum to let her know he was fine. She said she was pleased for him, although she did start crying, but he could tell she'd been drinking. He'd go and see her as soon as he could, he told himself, as long as Frank wasn't there.

He didn't see anything of Lem; the King of Crap Palace stayed upstairs. Robbie didn't want to bother him; everyone seemed to realise he was happier on his own. Kinard said he might come down to talk to Canner's new rescuee, Lucy, depending on how long it looked like she was going to stay. He might go out with her and Canner to get some fresh lights, or another gas bottle for the heaters. But Robbie guessed he'd make sure they didn't run out of petrol again.

Three days passed, and Robbie was starting to get used to the peculiar rhythm of warehouse life. He settled, he calmed. Although he spent plenty of time by himself, he never actually felt alone. And that mattered. The bruising on his face and ribs had started to fade. His fingers looked as though they were going to heal, albeit awkwardly.

Canner was impressed. 'Looks like you're permanently telling the world to sit on this and swivel,' he said approvingly.

So the weekend came and on the Saturday night Robbie saw his brother again.

He'd been talking more and more with Stef these last few days, and was growing to like her more and more. But that didn't mean he fancied her, no way. She was nineteen, and he knew that older girls never went out with younger boys, so there wasn't much point in fancying her anyway. Even if Canner had teased she had a soft spot for him. Robbie thought she was really clever, but just because she was pretty underneath her purple dreadlocks and nose-rings, it didn't mean he fancied her.

He hadn't forgotten that he'd promised to repay her for the apples she let him have on his first morning and had bought half a dozen of the juiciest-looking Granny Smiths he could find. He knew The Breech on Danes Street, the pub where she worked, and decided to meet her with them as a surprise. He hoped they could walk back to the warehouse together after she'd finished work.

She'd certainly been shocked when he'd appeared and waved the bag of apples at her, but that had been the idea, and the look of surprise on her face had been exactly as Robbie had imagined it: perfect.

'Who's this, then?' Terry, the landlord, had asked her. He seemed gruff, but tolerant. He was almost as big as Kinard, but it was mostly gut. 'This your boyfriend, is it?'

'I don't think so,' Stef laughed, shaking her head. 'More like my younger brother, aren't you, Robbie?'

He'd nodded quickly, managing not to look disappointed. Because he didn't fancy her.

He'd been worried the landlord might kick him out for being under age, but Terry had said: 'I don't mind you staying as long as you stick with the Coke.'

Robbie sat on a tall stool at the end of the bar nearest the juke-box, his feet not touching the floor, and watched the customers through the heavy cigarette smoke. It was an old-fashioned pub, not like the loud, wanna-be trendy bars that had sprung up all over the town centre, and quiet even on this Saturday night. Most of the regulars were old blokes in jumpers like George, who all knew each other; none of them had their wives with them. There was only one table of younger people – three lads and their girlfriends laughing loudly in the corner together – but then the juke-box only played what Canner would call typical middle-of-the-road cack. But Stef seemed to enjoy herself, and knew a lot of the customers by name. Sometimes they didn't even have to tell her which drink they wanted. Robbie watched her work, thinking how nice she looked in her white blouse with her dreadlocks pulled back in a ponytail. Terry left her alone at the bar and Robbie thought it must be nice to have that sort of responsibility and be trusted.

She rang the bell at ten to eleven for last orders and Robbie needed the loo after drinking five glasses of Coke one after another. His teeth felt slimy with it, and his stomach ached with the gas. He was quick in the toilets, wondering whether he should offer to help Stef clear up, but when he walked back into the bar he saw his brother leaning over the pumps, drunkenly counting out change into Stef's hand.

It was as if he'd walked into an invisible wall, a force-field. His feet simply stopped working and he stood in the door-way, unable to move a single centimetre further. Frank was wearing his favourite shirt, the green designer one, and it was unbuttoned at the neck so that you could see his thick gold chain. He must have been on his way home from another pub because it was obvious he'd already had a skin-full: his face was slack with it. He dropped some of his money on the floor and took an age to bend down to pick it up. His limbs were loose, his knees threatening to buckle any second. His neck looked as though it was made of jelly the way his head bobbed and wobbled. Robbie had seen him in this state many times before. He knew it often preceded a beating.

He felt a rush of sickness. He tried to tell himself it was all that Coke, but he knew it was because he was frightened of his brother. Stef glanced up and frowned, puzzled to see him standing there, and that gave him the push he needed to get back out into the corridor and then the toilets. He locked himself in a cubicle.

He didn't know who to hate more, himself or his brother. His fingers hadn't bothered him much the last day or two, but they were beginning to hurt again now and he held them to his chest. He hated his brother for making him feel so young and weak. In the warehouse he was as old as he wanted to be and he felt mature. He had a job; he had older friends. But as soon as he saw Frank he was the timid little kid again, scared again, hiding again. And he hated himself for it.

He wondered if Frank was alone, or whether he had friends with him. Because that was a question Robbie had asked himself more and more often recently. He wanted to know what Frank was like when he wasn't at home. He worked as a security guard, and Robbie wanted to know what he was like with the people he worked with. Did he push them around? Did he try to intimidate them too? Or was it just Robbie?

Did Frank have any friends?

He sat in the locked cubicle and his fear gave way to this need to know what kind of person his brother really was. He cradled his fingers and it suddenly became very important to him.

He stepped out of the cubicle and paced up and down the toilets. He couldn't explain why; he couldn't find the words inside his head to express what he meant, but he needed to know if Frank had any friends.

'Robbie!' It was Stef. 'Robbie? Are you in there?' She poked her head round the door. 'Are you okay?'

He nodded, still pacing.

'You looked kind of, you know . . . funny.'

He caught a glimpse of himself in the smeared and dirty

mirror above the hand basins, and was amazed to see his strained, pop-eyed expression.

Stef was watching him carefully. 'Come on, what's wrong?'

First of all he'd been frozen to the spot; now he couldn't keep still. He managed to force his feet to stop. 'D'you know that lad you just served . . .?'

She nodded. 'Frank? What about him?'

'You know him!'

'Well, yeah. He's always in here for last orders. Always hammered. Terry doesn't like him, says he's got a loud mouth and that he causes trouble with the regulars.'

'He's my brother,' Robbie told her, and saw the way her face creased as she tried to get a hold of the fact. 'What's he like?' he asked.

Stef had obviously been knocked off balance. 'I don't know. He's . . . Well, he's a bit of a prat if you ask me. But I never knew he . . .'

'Has he got any friends?'

'I don't know. He's usually on his own, I think.' Her face was hardening as she put two and two together. 'Look, do you want me to tell Terry?'

'No.' Robbie shook his head fiercely. 'No. I just need to know if he's got any friends.'

Again, Stef was at a loss. 'What do you mean?'

He was going to try and explain it to her, but angry voices suddenly erupted from the bar. Shouted threats and swearing, glass smashed. She swore and ran to see what was going on. Robbie was close behind her, his heart speeding up.

A table had been overturned, stools knocked over, shattered glass and spilled beer on the carpet. Everybody was on their feet. Their raised voices and angry shouts were aimed at Frank, who was standing in the centre of it all, his fists clenched. He swayed the tiniest amount, and although his face was flushed red with booze, his eyes were sharp and hard like glass.

'You want a piece? Come on then, if you want to have a go!'

He was facing down one of the younger lads Robbie had seen with their girlfriends earlier. And although this other lad was taller than Frank, he didn't look the fighting kind. He tried to look as though he could hold his own, wanting to stand his ground with his girlfriend watching, but he couldn't match Frank's spite.

'Just apologise to my girlfriend,' he was saying. The girl herself had a dark stain down the front of her T-shirt and an empty glass. 'Buy her another drink, that's all I'm asking you to do – there doesn't need to be any trouble.'

Frank swayed like a cobra.

Robbie had seen that look in his brother's eyes too many times to remember. He knew the other lad didn't stand a chance.

'I'm going to get Terry from upstairs,' Stef said and disappeared behind the bar to fetch the landlord.

None of the regulars was trying to help. It was just a show to them.

Frank was getting impatient. He had geared himself up for a fight and wasn't going to leave without having a piece. 'Come on,' he was saying. 'Come on, then,' trying to goad the other lad into making a move, into sealing his own fate. 'You want some, do you?'

One of the lad's friends stepped forward, trying to diffuse things. He wore glasses, which he pushed up his nose, smiling, trying to appear agreeable. 'Look, let's just get another drink, okay? We can—' He put a hand on Frank's shoulder, and it was all the excuse Robbie's brother needed.

He struck out, a dull crack as the punch connected. The lad's glasses exploded from his face, his head snapped back on his neck. He went down. Violence had focused Frank's every move. From the shambling drunk fumbling for change he'd transformed into a controlled and precise thug. It didn't matter that this wasn't who he'd originally had the quarrel with. He didn't care. It didn't even cross his mind. He kicked the lad when he was down, knowing exactly where to place his boot as the lad squirmed desperately to protect himself.

Seeing it from the outside for the first time shook Robbie. A single step from what was happening somehow made it very clear what he himself had been through so many times.

Now people were trying to break it up. The regulars were grabbing at Frank. One of the girls tried to pull her boyfriend away. 'Call the police,' she was shouting. 'Get the police.' The lad's friends were stepping in between, shouldering Frank backwards, away. One of them slammed a punch into his stomach, doubling him over, making him gasp for breath. He tried to swing back, but both of them were on him. Frank was the one on the floor now, fending off the blows.

Terry the landlord appeared. He and two of the bigger regulars soon had hold of Frank and the two lads. They were dragged out of the bar, out into the street.

Robbie followed them. He saw his brother wilt. As soon as the aggression was gone the drink took over again. He stumbled and staggered as Terry shoved him from behind, as if those feet which had been so exact with their kicks could no longer move quick enough to keep up.

'If you want to finish this, then you take it well away from my pub,' Terry warned them. 'You listening?'

Robbie knew the lads *were* determined to finish the beating. They were breathing hard, eager to lay into Frank as hard as he'd done to them. But Robbie realised he couldn't let them do it.

'Don't. Leave him. Leave him alone. He's my brother.'

'You what?' The one who'd been Frank's original target was flushed and tense. He wanted revenge. 'Did you see what he did to my mate in there?'

Frank looked up at Robbie, seeing him for the first time, and sneered. 'As if I need my soap-dodging little brother sticking up for me,' he slurred. He tried to square himself up, ready for another go, but his energy was spent; quick and fast, exploded like a bomb.

Terry eyed Robbie carefully, then nodded and said: 'You two, inside.' He ordered the lads back into his pub. 'Go get your girlfriends. But if I hear one peep out of you then I'll finish this myself. I'm locking the doors –' he hooked a thumb at Frank – 'and I'll let you out when this waste of space has crawled back under his rock.' He turned to Frank now. 'You're barred. I don't need your custom, and will manage without it fine enough from now on. If I catch you in my pub again I won't be happy – not happy at all. Understand?' Finally he said to Robbie: 'Are you staying with your brother? No? Then you'd better come inside too.'

Frank's drunken mind slowly realised what had happened. 'Hey. Hey! I don't need him sticking up for me.' He shoved Robbie away, but it was weak. He tried to grab one of the lads. 'Come on, you little prick!' he shouted. 'Come on. Let's finish it then.' He staggered, only just managed to keep his balance and stay on his feet. 'I thought you wanted some. *Come on!*' He shouted and bellowed, thumped on the door as Terry closed it on him. Robbie saw his twisted and spiteful face as he was locked out, no longer tough or intimidating, just nasty like a bullying child.

Stef was sweeping up the broken glass in the bar. The table and chairs had been righted. Terry marched the lads back over and told them they didn't leave until Frank was well away, and then they weren't welcome back in his pub again either.

'What happened?' Stef wanted to know.

'He might not be your boyfriend,' Terry said, nodding at Robbie, 'but he's a sensible lad. You could do worse.'

Stef looked confused. 'What?'

'I just didn't want to see my brother get beaten up,' Robbie said.

Stef didn't look as though that answer helped any. 'Even after everything he's done to you?'

Robbie shrugged. He still didn't know how to put it into words exactly, but he knew now that it wasn't just him his brother threatened and lashed out at. And that mattered.

If he'd only ever bullied Robbie, if it had only ever been Robbie on the receiving end of his fists, then it had to have been solely about their dad. Everything would have been about their dad leaving them and Frank blaming Robbie for what he did when he was eight.

Maybe things would have been different if their dad hadn't left them – maybe, but it was too late now. Tonight Robbie had seen that Frank was exactly the same whether he was at home or not, whether Robbie was on the receiving end or not.

He struggled to say something that Stef would understand. 'Frank hasn't got any friends,' he told her. 'He hates every-body, not just me.'

And that was what mattered most.

AMY AGAINST THE WORLD

One

Amy clutched the telephone so tightly, she had it pressed so hard against her ear, that the back of her earring stabbed into the tender flesh behind her lobe. Not that she would notice until long after she'd slammed the phone down and left the phone box.

She was trying to form a picture of the thief's face inside her head by listening to the sound of his voice. She was keeping him talking. It was so important to her to know what he looked like. But he was speaking with a false accent, his voice a cruel imitation of her own. It was an extra purposeful twist of the knife, an added humiliation. She hated him for it.

'I have nothing left,' she told him. Again. 'You have to understand . . .'

The amusement in his voice set her teeth on edge. 'I'm *so* sorry, my dear, but I'm afraid I have another appointment to keep. Thank you for calling.' He blew her a kiss. A cartoonish smackeroo ending in a wet pop. 'Chin up, and cheery-bye for now.'

She couldn't hold down the surge of panic. 'No! Wait! Please. I have to have my things back. You can keep my money, okay? But, please, my clothes, my passport. I need . . .' But she was talking to herself.

For a few seconds she felt breathless, like a rock-climber whose one and only rope snaps, sending them tumbling into free-fall. She closed her eyes against the dizziness, biting hard on her bottom lip until it passed.

If she were a rock-climber, however, she'd cling on till the bitter end, rope or no rope. Until her fingernails finally broke or the cliff face fell away. Parents, teachers and friends had all condemned her for her stubbornness too many times to remember, and yet she'd always preferred to see it as one of her more positive traits.

She re-dialled the number of her mobile phone.

And listened to it ring.

She had a picture of the thief in her mind now. She could see his heavy eyebrows and the long blade of nose she imagined him to have. She could see his thin lips and an ugly arrogance in the way he smiled. She could see his glittering blue eyes. She thought he must have beautiful, intelligent eyes: all sparkles. Full of self-confidence and the belief that he was the cleverest man on the planet.

He wasn't answering. Her mobile phone rang and rang. Then her own recorded voice kicked in, asking so politely for her to leave a message. She could hear the elocution lessons her mother had forced her to have when she was seven and realised just how accurately spiteful the thief's imitation was.

She banged the receiver down into its cradle. Thought about it for a second. Then snatched it up and banged it down again. She kicked her way out of the phone box. The tears were close and threatening but she shook her head hard, shook them away.

The high street was busy; people stared at her as they bustled by with their shopping bags. A little boy wearing a Teletubbies T-shirt gazed at her with undisguised curiosity, until his mother tugged at his hand and hurried him along. There was a long queue at the bus stop on the opposite side of the road. Amy was suddenly the main attraction.

She stepped back into the relative safety of the telephone box, ignoring as best she could the fact of its glass sides. And dialled her number again.

She let it ring, listened to her message, then dialled again. Listened. Dialled again.

Now the thief had switched her phone off so it didn't even ring any more – her recorded message jumped in straight away. She felt a small, cold thrill of pleasure at that. Getting on his nerves, was she? What a pity! She left a message of screeched four-letter words. Then, lifting the receiver high above her head with both hands, clenching her jaw until her teeth hurt, she slammed it down one last time with as much force as she could muster.

The telephone didn't return any change.

She shouldered the door open, pushing out onto the street. She walked with her head held high, looking right through anyone who stared at her. She walked quickly, but she caught a glimpse of herself in Woolworths' window: her long blonde ponytail dark with grease, her slept-in T-shirt and rumpled jeans, the traces of two-day-old make-up on her face. And suddenly she was staring at her feet, hurrying now, feeling embarrassed. Feeling strung-out. Feeling hot and dirty. Angry. Stupid. Exhausted, scared, alone . . .

Now the tears came. She honestly didn't think she had any left, but here came more. She kept her head down, not wanting anyone seeing her in this state, even strangers. Oh she hated this, hated this! She refused to look up from her feet as she hurried, half-running, stumbling a little to avoid bumping into anyone – as if she had the plague and was scared she might pass it on. It was as though the whole world was watching her, and shaking their heads and tutting.

She turned off the high street towards the little town-centre park she'd passed that morning. The sun pressed down on her with a clammy palm and she headed for the shade of some trees. She found a bench underneath a tall horse chestnut and collapsed back onto it.

More tears.

She fought against them, sniffing, swallowing hard. No more, she told herself. Last time; no more. With a deep breath she sat upright, back straight, head high, chin up. She honestly wasn't someone who cried a lot; she'd certainly never been the self-pitying type. Another deep breath, gently brushing away any wetness from under her eyes with the tips of her fingers. In her first year at secondary school she'd beaten Stephen Weston in a fight while all the kids from her class had watched open-mouthed. She was tougher than she looked. Just sometimes not tough enough, obviously.

Everything was such a mess.

She had a single pound coin left. That was all. One pound. She dug it out of her jeans pocket and stared at it. She listed everything she could do with it, trying to make it sound positive. Did one pound or one hundred pence sound more optimistic?

She could buy something to eat, maybe. As a matter of fact, she *should* buy something to eat. She was sure part of the reason she felt so tired and light-headed was because she hadn't eaten yet today. Or she could find the local swimming baths and have a shower. She'd love a shower. Even without soap or shampoo.

She could phone her parents, and admit to them what had happened. She knew they'd help. They'd stop this mess in an instant, she knew that. Her father would quite literally leap into the car and break every speeding law on the motorway down from Durham to save his little girl. But she also knew what he'd say, and how he'd treat her. Like a clumsy, naïve child. Like the prissy-in-pink, pig-tailed poppet from the family album. She couldn't stand that. She'd lose ten years in a matter of seconds. She was eighteen now, but her father sometimes had difficulty admitting it. And when she got home the look of 'Told-you-so' righteous triumph on her mother's face would make her want to scream.

But at least it would all be over.

She closed her eyes as a tiny breeze moved through the shade of the tall tree, cooling her hot cheeks. She was supposed to be on a beach in Spain. She should be drinking wine in Rome.

It was her last pound coin. It was her last anything. Full stop.

She walked out of the park and back to the high street, back to the telephone box. She used the pound to call her mobile one more time, and left a message apologising for her outburst, asking the thief to reconsider, to please understand. Then she had nothing.

She made her way slowly and miserably back towards the warehouse, fingering the spot of blood behind her ear.

Two

The centre of the warehouse was where people met up in the evening to pass the time. They played cards and chatted, bathed in the glow of stolen workmen's lights. There was usually a radio playing, and tonight was no different.

There were perhaps as many as a dozen people hanging around tonight. They sat on broken plastic seats or squatted on the bare floor. The air above them was a steady haze of cigarette smoke. One of the few not smoking was the sandy-haired boy Shelly pointed out.

'That's him,' she told Amy.

The boy looked up. 'I'm him who?'

Amy felt strangely tentative. 'Are you the Can-I Man?'

He jumped up from his chair. 'Close enough,' he said, with a huge face-splitting smile that actually made Amy take a small step backwards. He stood and beamed at her expectantly.

She was very conscious of the group of people sitting around. 'And you can get things?'

It should have been physically impossible, but his grin spread wider. 'I certainly can. What is it you're after?'

Amy hesitated. It was obvious everybody was listening, even if they were pretending not to.

'She wants a guitar,' Shelly piped up. 'She wants to go busking.'

Curious faces actually turned towards her now, and Amy frowned at Shelly, who simply shrugged.

Shelly had been the first person from the warehouse

Amy had met when she'd arrived two days ago, and at the moment they were sharing a kip. She wasn't the type of girl Amy would usually choose as a friend. She was loud and garish and claimed her most prized possession was her black Wonderbra. She reminded Amy of a cheap Christmas tree bauble. She wasn't particularly pretty, but she was the kind of girl who'd never be short of a boyfriend or two, because boys seemed to like all that surface glitter. But on Tuesday Amy really hadn't been in any position to refuse a helping hand from anyone. It had been the worst day of her life ever.

The sandy-haired boy was surprised by the request. His smile concertinaed as he pursed his lips. 'Guitars aren't my hottest subject,' he admitted. 'I'm guessing it's something specific you're after.'

'She just wants to go busking,' Shelly reiterated, in a voice that would scare rhinoceroses.

Amy cringed. 'Can we talk about it somewhere a little bit more . . .?'

The lad nodded. 'I'm following you.'

Of course nowhere in the warehouse could be called truly private. Amy found this particularly difficult. If there was anything she needed more than most, it was her space. The only place they could go was back to the kip, hoping Shelly didn't follow along. Some of the other kips looked like proper rooms (almost) but the one she shared with Shelly was simply separated from everybody else by a couple of curtains which could be pulled across and staked out, like an awning. There was room enough behind the curtains for two lumpy mattresses. Shelly had a sleeping bag, but Amy had had to sleep in her clothes. She had never felt so grubby or claustrophobic in her life before.

'I expect people will be talking about me now,' she said. She didn't turn to look at the lad following her. 'I'll be the snooty cow who wants everybody to mind their own business.'

'I doubt it,' he said. 'The nice thing about this place is that we all have more than enough of our own business to mind anyway. What's your name by the way?'

She did consider a lie, but: 'Amy.'

'I'm Canner. Or the Can Man. Or even the *Can-I* Man, if you prefer.'

'Why?'

'Why what?'

'Why are you called Canner or whatever?'

'Because if you want something,' he said proudly, reciting a line he'd repeated many times before (just as proudly), 'I can get it.'

Amy had met his type before. She'd met them all before. He was a geek, a loser, but in this place full of losers he liked to think of himself as someone important. 'Is it your real name?'

'It's what everybody calls me, so it's real enough as far as I'm concerned.'

'And you steal things?'

'I take charitable donations from people who don't realise how generous they're being.'

'Which is stealing, yes?'

He eyed her carefully. She smiled back at him. 'I never sell anything,' he told her. 'I never make a profit.'

She didn't drop her smile; even though her teeth were getting cold. 'But basically you steal things?'

'Only from those who already *have* things.' He shook his head at her. 'Give me a break. I'm meant to be one of the good guys.'

'Did you use to be Robin Hood in a former life?'

He nodded quickly, beaming his smile again. 'Yeah,' he said. 'Yeah, probably. I've never thought of that before.' He laughed, even though Amy hadn't meant it to be quite so funny. 'Robin *Hood*. I like that.'

She was the biggest hypocrite the world had ever seen, she knew that. She was stuck in this place because someone probably not unlike Canner had stolen from her, and yet now here she was asking him to steal *for* her. But losing a guitar was nothing compared to what she'd lost, she told herself. And if she was forced to stand up and fight for herself, then other people should be willing to do the same. Wasn't that what this stupid, messed-up world was all about?

The heavy curtain smelled fusty, like the dirty sheep on the farm Amy had visited once as a child. She pulled it aside and ducked underneath into the kip as quickly as she could, touching it as briefly as possible. Clothes were scattered all over Shelly's side, spilling out of two distressed carrier bags. A pair of outrageously colourful knickers had been dropped on Amy's mattress. She picked them up with fingers like tweezers before flinging them back onto Shelly's pile.

Canner was watching her carefully and gave a knowing little chortle.

She bristled. 'What?' she asked indignantly.

'You're not used to this communal living lark, I take it?'

She sat down on her mattress, drew up her knees and met his eye. 'I want a guitar, not sagacity.' She saw him frown at the big word and allowed herself a brief smile. If there was anything she'd learned from her mother, it was how to be a bitch. She might be stuck here for a few days, she might have to live with these people for now, but it didn't mean she had to join their band of merry men. Because she wasn't like them.

It was important to keep her distance. She wasn't looking for friends, she told herself. She didn't want any of them getting close. She didn't want to risk someone seeing inside her. They might see her shame, and how her empty stomach churned when she thought about what had happened to her.

So she told herself she had nothing in common with anyone here. Her being here was not a life-style choice.

Canner fidgeted from foot to foot. 'What kind of guitar is it you're after, then?'

'It's got to be acoustic,' she told him. 'I can't very well go busking with an electric one, can I? There's no sockets in the middle of the street, is there?'

She realised he was staring at her – in that way she recognised all too well. She'd had boys look at her like this before, of course. She'd had her fair share of boyfriends. She'd learned how to manipulate boys who looked at her like this, when she needed a fresh drink or someone to drive her home at the end of the night. But she knew how grotty and dishevelled she looked right now, and was quite honestly surprised by Canner's reaction. Perhaps she didn't look as bad as she'd thought. It had only been a brief glimpse in Woolworths' window after all. She sat up a little straighter. She'd have to check in the little mirror in Shelly's bag.

Although as soon as she met his gaze he flinched away. 'Acoustic. Right. D'you want a speaker or amplifier what'sit as well?' He hadn't been listening to a word she'd said. Like all boys. Too busy staring at her tits.

'No,' she said very slowly. 'That's why it's *acoustic*. It doesn't *need* amplification.'

He nodded quickly, head bobbing like a sewing machine. 'Of course. Yeah. You're right.' He gave a little laugh. 'That's *why* it's acoustic.'

They were quiet. There were two radios playing somewhere in the warehouse. They both stared around awkwardly at the dark curtains, the lumpy mattresses, Shelly's clothes.

'Is that all you want?' he eventually asked.

She narrowed her eyes. 'What do you mean?'

But before he could answer someone shouted: 'Canner! Patrol!'

He swore, and was instantly ducking out underneath the curtain. 'Turn the lights off,' he shouted. 'Get those radios off.'

Amy was on her feet too. She didn't follow, however, she stayed exactly where she was. She didn't want to be involved and didn't know what was happening anyway. She could hear Canner running towards the centre. Then the orange glow from the lights dimmed, dimmed, went out and the whole warehouse was plunged into blackness.

It was the first time it had ever been completely dark since she'd been here. They usually left one or two of the lights on, which she found strangely comforting. Now, however, she couldn't see her hand in front of her face. She stood very still. Her shared kip, surrounded only by the fusty curtain, was now suddenly fragile and unsafe.

There was a radio playing somewhere in the darkness. A shout rang out. 'Whose is that radio?' 'We've got a patrol!' Canner's voice now. 'Turn it off!' But it played on.

Someone stumbled past in the dark; there was a banging on a wooden wall. 'Turn it off! Turn it off!'

Then silence, as though the warehouse itself was holding its breath. Amy dared to move: feeling behind her for her mattress she lowered herself slowly down. She sat and hugged her knees to her chest. She was frightened. What was happening? She strained her ears for any sound other than the heavy thumping of her heart. Why didn't somebody tell her what was happening?

She waited in the dark, trying to breathe as shallowly and as quietly as possible. The world could have stopped. She rocked herself a little.

It might be just like this when you die.

Somebody brushed past the curtain with a swish against the cloth and she had to bite back a scream.

'It's only me,' she heard Canner say from the darkness. Then: 'Okay. They've gone,' he shouted. 'Can someone turn the lights back on?'

Slowly the orange glow brightened to illuminate the warehouse and the inside of the kip. The two radios started up again as if nothing had happened.

Canner poked his head in through the curtains. 'You okay?'

'What happened?'

He came all the way inside again. 'It was a couple of security guards. They're not too much of a worry really, but they come by every couple of weeks to nose around the docks, and we'd rather they didn't find us here. For obvious reasons. They never hang around or come in downstairs or anything, but if they did they'd certainly hear any moron who kept his radio playing.' His face was reddened and angry.

'Whose was it?' she asked quietly. She couldn't help being a little unsettled by Canner's transformation from geek to Action Man in the blink of an eye. A few minutes ago she thought she'd had him pinned down, sussed out.

'That American bloke,' he said. 'I don't know his name. D'you know him?'

She shook her head. She hadn't met anyone apart from Shelly, because of wanting to keep her distance.

'He came in on Tuesday, same day as you, that was all. Or maybe it was Monday. Not that it matters.' He puffed out his breath and shrugged, moving on. 'Anyway, what I was saying was, tell me if there's anything else I can get for you. Apart from the guitar, I mean.'

'Why?' She was still sitting hugging her knees to her chest, still shaken by what had happened. This place and the people in it distressed her. Whatever kind of place it was, secret and hiding from patrols. Whoever the runaways and villains and Robin Hood wannabes were who lived here.

Canner half-gestured at Shelly's mattress and the battered carrier bags stuffed with clothes. Amy was acutely aware that she had nothing but the clothes she was wearing. She ran a hurried hand through her lank, greasy hair, grimaced at the feel of it. She realised Canner had probably been staring at her because of the godawful state she was in. No other reason. How ridiculous she must have looked. How very pathetic.

She was quite proud of herself when she came up with the idea of busking to raise some money. She couldn't face begging – the thought depressed her. Scared her. This way was clever, she told herself. And this way wasn't giving in.

She'd loathed her guitar lessons as a child, had used every excuse in the book to avoid practising. Yet now she'd decided it was the perfect way to get some money together to buy food, perhaps even clothes. And if all she raised was enough for a train ticket home, then at least she hadn't had to call her parents. She could go home more or less on her own terms. Maybe not with her head held high, but at least with a little pride and independence left intact. Although now she sat with her head down, feeling dirtier and more out of place than ever.

Perhaps she wasn't so different from the other people here. Perhaps just being in the warehouse was commonality enough.

The hateful tears threatened, but she was strong enough to hold them back. She closed her eyes on them. It was turning out to be a never-ending battle. 'I've had everything stolen,' she said simply. 'Everything.'

'Let me get you what I can,' he said. 'I've got a blanket you can have, at least.'

She wouldn't look at him. She hugged her knees tighter than ever. 'Why would you want to?' She'd never met anyone who did things for free. Not where she came from. Oh yes, she could persuade boys to buy her drinks or drive her home, but they always wanted something in return. She wondered what this Can Man would want. The boys at home could be pushy enough; the fact that people in the warehouse seemed to work on an altogether more ambiguous level scared her. 'You don't even know me. Why should you bother?'

He blinked twice, thinking about it only briefly. 'Because I'm one of the good guys, obviously.'

THREE

Sheffield train station had been packed and bustling when Amy arrived there about midday on Tuesday morning. The platforms had been crowded, the footbridges choked with passengers and their luggage. The announcer's voice had been shrill and unintelligible; the timetables could easily have been written in Egyptian, with their odd little pictograms and seemingly random numbers. Amy had walked around a little cloudy and dazed, apologising to every other person she passed because she kept bumping into them with the cumbersome rucksack she carried on her back. She'd told herself she now realised why tortoises always looked so naffed off with the world.

On the train she'd had mixed feelings of excitement and trepidation. Her first holiday without her parents, her first holiday alone; she had an Inter-rail ticket promising a month's worth of travel throughout Europe. She was going to see Paris, Prague, and probably everywhere else. Unfortunately these feelings had quickly rolled over to show their underbelly of embarrassment and frustration when she realised she was on the wrong train. Which was why she'd ended up in Sheffield, when she should have been well on her way to London. Then Dover, then abroad.

She blamed her mother, who'd caused a scene back at Durham station, forcing Amy to jump on the first train she saw just to get away from it. Neither of her parents was happy about her travelling by herself. They'd wasted several good trees' worth of breath trying to convince her not to go. Especially after Juliet had let her down.

It had been the two of them together at first, their big best-friends' adventure before uni kicked off in October. Had been. Until Juliet had started fawning over Josh Gregory. With what Amy now considered an unsurprising predictability he'd managed to persuade Juliet into going to Ibiza with him and his dead-head friends instead. His whining and pleading and sad-dog face had made Amy want to puke. When Juliet broke the news – over the phone because she didn't have the guts to say anything eye to eye – Amy's parents had redoubled their efforts of dissuasion. Her father in his gentle, caring, patronising way; her mother in her own unique fashion: 'Let's be honest, darling. You're far too clumsy to manage. You've never had to think for yourself before – why on earth would you want to start now?'

She was doing this to prove her mother wrong. She wanted to feel as though she was different to most of the other girls at school. She just wanted to be let off the leash a little. And yet her very first step had been a wrong one.

Sheffield!

She had fought her way through the crowds, trying to listen to the announcer, straining in case she could hear the word 'London'. Her shoulders and the back of her neck ached something chronic from the huge rucksack. She spied an empty bench at the end of the platform and waded through the bustle towards it. Her muscles sang with relief when she swung the ridiculous pack off her shoulders and was able to flop down onto the bench next to it.

Okay, she told herself. No big disaster in the great scheme of things, so no panicking. Sheffield was still closer to London than Durham.

She'd been sweating and took off her new rainproof, pulling it over her head. She was wearing all new clothes; she'd played on her father's anxieties to get him to fork out for only the best. Loose canvas jeans, cropped T-shirt, walking boots. All appropriately labelled. Her hair was tied back in what she thought was a rather perky ponytail, with a headscarf which in her mind added that authentic back-packer touch. She checked in the rainproof's pockets. Money, yes. Passport, yes. See? Everything. She folded it up and pushed it inside the top of her rucksack. As soon as there was a train to London she'd be back on track – literally. What was a lost hour when she had four weeks? She'd look back at this and laugh.

And that was the moment when she'd spotted the man in the railway uniform amongst the crowd. 'Excuse me!' She leapt up from the bench. 'Excuse me!' She'd had to run a few steps to catch his arm. 'Hello . . . hi. Hi there. Can you tell me when the next train to London is due, please?'

He seemed particularly efficient. He checked his watch and said: 'Next one's in ten minutes. Platform Four.'

'Thank you.' She gave him her bestest smile, because thanks to him everything was going to be okay again.

But when she'd turned back to the bench her rucksack had gone.

She'd replayed those few seconds over and over in her head many, many times since. She'd tried to alter time and events by sheer force of will. She'd pulled each second apart, dissected them, studied them, rearranged them to make the outcome more palatable. If only she had . . . Perhaps she could have . . . She'd tormented herself with an endless string of possibilities which all began 'What if . . .'

But nothing would ever change what had actually happened.

She'd stared at the bench, at the exact spot where her ruck-sack had been only seconds before. It hadn't reappeared. Not even when she'd raced back over and stood there. Not even when her belly had slowly filled with an almost liquid cold.

She turned on the spot, frantically looking around,

searching the swarm of people. Her eyes skittered through them. She wanted them all to stand still. If everybody stood still then maybe she could . . . Maybe it would . . .

No.

But it had been so *heavy*. It had been so bloody heavy and cumbersome. Who the hell could have picked it up so easily? Who would dare? Who would dare to steal her rucksack?

What followed had been the worst afternoon of her life. There'd been tears in the station manager's office, tears in front of the transport police, tears in lost property. She'd been left with the clothes she was wearing and the £10 note in her jeans pocket. Everything else – *everything*, EVERYTHING – had gone.

Whoever she'd spoken to had told her to call her parents, but they'd all acted and sounded like her parents too. She'd thought the woman in lost property might actually pat her on the head and call her 'poppet'. She hadn't been able to explain to them, but she'd been holding back from making that phone call. The *very* last resort, nothing else. Because this was supposed to be her being grown-up, her being independent. Not her being in the wrong train station and having EVERYTHING stolen. It was exactly as her mother had predicted. For Amy this had been her one and only chance to prove her wrong.

The afternoon had crept along in a slow blur. Just a fog full of empty holes; nothing she could see to do to make things better. By early evening she'd found herself back on the bench with her head in her hands, because there simply wasn't anywhere else for her to go. She was coming to the conclusion that all she was doing was prolonging the agony before she would have to make that call home. She'd noticed somebody sitting next to her, but didn't look up until he spoke.

'Are you okay?' he asked. He was unshaven, dark-haired, about her age, and lazily dressed in a pale, short-sleeved shirt and cargo pants. He looked like the backpacker she'd hoped to fool the world she was too.

She hadn't answered him. She'd given him a glare which quite clearly said, 'Do I look like it?!'

'Have you got somewhere to go?' he asked. He could have been a weirdo or pervert or anything.

She was too washed-out and exhausted to care. 'You work it out. Do you think I'd be sitting here if I did?'

He didn't react to her venom. 'I know a place you can go,' he told her.

He was called Matty. He'd bought her a coffee and told her about the warehouse he'd just come from: a place where she could stay as long as she wanted, no questions asked. He'd not mocked her suspicions, simply assured her it was safe. And maybe it had been her desperation and how dog-tired she felt. Or maybe it had been because there simply didn't seem to be any need for him to lie, no matter which way she looked at it. So she'd trusted him.

He explained that he'd originally bought himself a return ticket, but had decided during the journey to Sheffield that he was moving on for good this time, so he let her have it. He'd called Shelly and arranged for her to meet Amy at the station when she arrived. He'd also told her that if she needed anything, anything at all, someone called Canner would be able to help her.

Amy had caught the train to the small town she'd never even heard of before. Matty had given her Shelly's mobile number in case there was a problem, and that had made her think about her own mobile tucked into the side pocket of her rucksack. It was a top-of-the-range WAP phone which she could have used abroad; her father had insisted on it. As soon as she got off the train, before meeting Shelly, she'd called herself from the nearest phone box.

The thief answered after the second ring.

Now, on Friday, three days after her rucksack had been stolen, she'd spent every last penny of her £10 note calling him.

Last night she'd asked Canner for a guitar. She hoped with her whole being that he could back up his big mouth and bluster and get her one. This morning she'd sold her earrings for a pathetic £5. She hadn't been able to find a pawn shop or a second-hand jewellers, but a lady working at a cheap accessory stall on the market had taken pity on her. Amy hadn't admitted the gold studs were worth ten times as much. She just wanted the money to call him again.

'Well, well,' he cooed in that smug imitation of her accent, raising the hackles on her neck. 'If it isn't my foul-mouthed friend again.'

'I apologised,' she said quickly. 'I left you a message apologising.'

'I'm not sure I can forgive you, Amy.' His voice dripped slime. 'I was extremely upset by those names you called me.'

Even with its glass-panel sides the phone box was claustrophobic. She had her eyes closed tight, her picture of him in her mind. There was a lump of gorge in her throat that she struggled to swallow down. 'Please listen. You've got to tell me where you are.' She'd lain awake most of last night planning what to say to him. 'If you're still in Sheffield you can just leave my rucksack in the train station's lost property. You won't get caught. You'll still be anonymous.'

'Anonymous, eh? Now there's a good word.' In her mind his sharp blue eyes glittered like a conceited magician's. 'And what if I'm not in Sheffield any more?'

'Any train station will do. I'll find my way there. Please, you've got everything I own. My clothes and everything.'

'I know.' He wasn't being boastful.

She gripped the receiver. She was boiling with suppressed anger. She took a breath to keep control. She was desperate to let it out at him, to tell him exactly what she thought of him. Last night, however, she'd decided the only way forward was to gain his sympathy. 'I'm homeless and penniless because you've . . .'

'Daddy phoned.'

Her words dried, turned solid in her mouth.

'He phones as often as you do, wanting to know how you are. He sounds like a *jolly nice fellow*, I must say. But he does sound worried.'

'What . . .? What have you said to him?' It came out as a cold whisper.

'I've told him I'm your new boyfriend, and that we're very much in love. That we'll soon be eloping to Vegas to get married. He wasn't willing to give us his blessing right away, admittedly. But I'm thinking he'll come round in the end.'

Amy was silent. A tide of nausea rolled over her: guilt and shame and fear. All in one huge, breaking wave.

'I spoke to your mother dearest too.' He paused, as if waiting for Amy to say something. She couldn't get her mouth to work. He carried on regardless. 'She annoyed me and I had to hang up. Je-sus, what a bitch! I found your Inter-rail ticket and do you know what I thought? I thought, No wonder Amy wants to get away for a month. Your mother never heard of Prozac?' His accent had slipped, but Amy was in no fit state to notice.

The pips sounded.

There was a sob trapped in Amy's throat. 'Please . . . I . . .'

After only a second or two the line went dead, the £5 all gobbled up by the greedy phone.

She gently replaced the receiver. Why hadn't she called her parents? What was she doing here? Why was this happening to her? She stood in the phone box for what seemed like a very long time.

FOUR

Rock bottom is firmer than you'd expect. Or so Amy decided. There is no lower. It's impossible to fall any further. This is what she told herself; it sounded convincing.

Friday night she retreated to the kip early because now more than ever she didn't want to spend time in the centre with anyone else. She didn't want to talk, or listen, or even bother. Shelly tried to prod her into life at one point, asking her if she wanted anything, but Amy pretended she was sleeping. She lay under her thin blanket on her bare mattress and curled herself up around her misery. She could smell herself, meaty, like old hamburgers. Her new clothes were now stretched and shapeless. She was worse than a tramp. She had hunger pangs, but it was the guilt that kept her awake for such a long time. She knew her parents wouldn't be sleeping either.

How stubborn could one person be before it drove them completely insane?

Too far, she told herself. She'd gone too far.

She decided she was going home. She'd phone her parents and allow them to come and rescue her. Not that the decision was in any way comforting. She hated the thought of having to give in, hated herself for not having the gumption or the balls.

But on that Saturday morning, when she woke with a thick head and heavy eyes, it was the Can Man who saved her. He gave her a beautiful guitar.

The fitful night was still fuzzy in her head, and she stood

outside the kip, holding the guitar as if it was the most fragile piece of glass, not knowing what on earth to say. Because it *was* a beautiful guitar. The pale-wood finish, the sparkle of the tuning pegs. She realised she had never been quite sure whether Canner could actually fulfil his boast. She'd never for a second dreamed he would deliver anything more than a tatty plank with washing-line for strings.

'Where . . .?' She stopped herself. Maybe it was better not to know. After such a horrible day yesterday, surely this was the boost she needed. This was like her prayers being answered from above. She'd sit and play outside Woolworths, the perfect spot, close to the bus stops. She'd soon raise some money. She'd call her parents. Then she could buy food. Soap and toothpaste and a clean pair of knickers. How like heaven clean undies sounded right now. She actually laughed out loud at the thought.

'Just one promise,' he said. 'No awkward questions, okay?'

She nodded quickly, slipping the strap over her head. She made the chord shapes, felt the action of the strings, tentatively strummed. 'I'm going to look just like Joni Mitchell.'

'Who?'

She laughed at him, but was suddenly cut short, and the guitar felt as heavy as a body around her neck. She remembered the small voice she'd heard inside her on Thursday night, but it was suddenly much louder now.

Canner's face was split by that ludicrous grin. He was so very pleased with himself. It was the so-very-smug, aren't-I-the-bee's-knees look on his face that made her turn away. She suddenly realised he had sparkling blue eyes; glittering, clever eyes. His eyes were the same as those she'd imagined for her thief.

And now she couldn't ignore that voice inside. She lifted the strap over her head. 'I can't accept this.' She held the guitar out to him.

His grin crumpled with the shock. 'It's yours. Isn't it what you wanted? I thought . . .'

'Take it back,' she said. 'I can't accept it.'

But he wouldn't take it from her. So she laid it on the floor at his feet and ducked back underneath the curtain into the kip.

He was quick to follow. 'I did what you wanted. It's acoustic, right? You can busk with it, can't you?'

She slumped down onto her mattress. 'It's a Gibson,' she said.

'And?'

'Do you know how much they cost?'

'You wanted a guitar. I got you a—'

'You got me one of the most expensive guitars going. You stole it without a second thought.' She threw her arms around the kip, a wild gesture forcing him to take it all in. 'See this? Look at me, look at what I've got. You were quite happy to point out my pitiful state the other night. And the only reason I'm stuck here is because someone like you stole everything I had.'

Canner couldn't have looked more hurt if she'd raked her nails across his face. Which annoyed her. Because it wasn't him who should be feeling hurt, but whoever had just lost their favourite guitar. He tried to pace up and down in his confusion, but the kip was far too small to allow it. He ended up hopping from foot to foot. He looked like a child who needed the toilet.

'I did what you asked. You asked can I get you a guitar, so I got you one. You were quite happy the other night, calling me Robin Hood and stuff.'

'Maybe things have changed.' Although she knew deep down she'd felt like a hypocrite even then.

He shrugged. 'Just like that.'

She stood her ground. 'Yes. Just like that.'

'How?'

She folded her arms, dared him to argue. 'I'm going home.'

Again the shocked look on his face. He shook his head and laughed through his nose. 'It's all right for those who can, I suppose.'

'What the hell's that supposed to mean?' She was ready to lash out at him with her nails for real now.

He held up his hands in surrender. And a sleep-furry voice from the other mattress said: 'Can't you do your arguing someplace else?' Neither of them had even considered Shelly, buried deep down in her sleeping bag.

But it wound Amy up even more. She felt a hot flash of anger: she couldn't go anywhere in this place without someone else being there, listening in, knowing her business. 'No, we can't go somewhere else!' she shouted. 'Because there's nowhere else *to* go. Is there?'

Shelly poked her head out. 'Has Lady Muck got her knickers stuck up her crack this morning, then?'

Amy was on her feet in an instant.

'Let's take a walk,' Canner said quickly, stepping between them.

Amy glared at Shelly, who returned a cool stare.

'Come on,' Canner said, trying to usher Amy out under the curtain.

She was reluctant, feeling perfectly willing right there and then to take out all her anger and frustration and guilt on Shelly. But Canner was insistent. He ducked out and held the curtain up for Amy to follow. She threw one more poisonous look in the other girl's direction before following.

'We'll go for a walk outside,' Canner said. He picked up the guitar and started making his way through the kips. 'Shelly's okay, you know. Loud, yes. But all right when you give her the chance.'

'Is that you taking sides then is it?' Amy asked nastily.

'She didn't have to meet you from the station. She was trying to help, because Matty asked her to. She doesn't have to share her kip with you.'

'If you say so.'

Canner shook his head at her. 'You're hard work, you are. Real high maintenance.'

Amy agreed unashamedly.

They headed out of the warehouse and onto the disused quayside. It was another warm morning, promising another beautiful day in the sunshine.

'I went to a lot of trouble to get you this guitar.' He still sounded more hurt than angry.

'So, *thank you*.'

He frowned at her.

She sighed deeply. 'I just can't accept it, can I?'

'Because?'

'Because then I'd be as bad as the arsehole who stole from me, wouldn't I?'

'Not necessarily,' he said defensively. 'But if you don't take it, you say you've to go home, right?'

'I've got no other way of making money. I refuse to beg.'

'So you're going to give up and go back home.'

She didn't like his tone of voice. She didn't like the way he'd managed to work out that going back home for her would be some kind of defeat. 'Maybe you and Shelly can live like this, in that place, but look at me. I'm not—'

'I don't want to know why you're here, but put it this way: I've not met anyone who came to the warehouse by accident. We're all here for a reason.'

'Very melodramatic. Do you also write scripts for *EastEnders*?'

He didn't acknowledge the insult, but she saw him stiffen the tiniest amount. He gripped the guitar by the neck and walked away along the water. He spoke quietly, forcing Amy to hurry to keep up if she wanted to hear what he was saying. 'So you go back home to the exact same problems that drove you away in the first place. I thought you were the type of person who—'

'Don't pretend to know me!'

For the second time that morning he held up his hands in surrender. 'Okay, so this is just my opinion. I'm not trying to tell you what to do or anything. Just what I reckon. Okay?'

She blew out a long, slow breath and planted her feet. If he was going to hold forth and moralise, or philosophise, or simply spout nonsense, he could do it without her running at his heels. But he didn't stop walking. And what pained her most of all was that she really did want to know what he had to say, because if he had a good reason for her not to go home she wanted to hear it. She gritted her teeth as she jogged a little to catch up.

'I reckon you've got to fight back,' he said. 'Unless you'd rather roll belly-up and give in. Up to you. But did you steal this guitar?'

She pulled a face at him. 'No. You did.'

'You don't know that for sure,' he told her. 'But you're probably right, I suppose. And I guess I could walk up and down here all day justifying what I do. I could tell you I only get people what they need to survive in the warehouse. That I never ask for monetary payment. That I only ever steal from people who can afford it—' He saw her about to speak. 'Not that I can ever prove that one hundred per cent, of course.' He waited until she'd closed her mouth again. 'But this is the way I look at it. This is my theory. Ready?'

'Come on, then!'

'I reckon I'm not going to heaven anyway,' he said, and carried on quickly before she had time to say anything. 'They would've never let me in whether I nicked this guitar or not.

I'm about as sinned-up as you can get, and that's why I'm so useful around here. I don't just help people out by getting them stuff they need, I also do them the service of keeping them guilt-free.'

She met his bright blue eyes. She saw the mischievous gleam. 'That's the biggest bag of bollocks I've ever heard.'

He laughed. 'Yeah, I thought so too. But I had you going for a while there, didn't I?'

She turned on her heel and stormed away. She didn't know whether to scream at him or laugh right along too. Who did he think he was, messing about with her like this?

Now it was his turn to run to catch up. 'Listen. Sorry . . . Wait up a minute.'

She slowed almost imperceptibly.

'Listen . . .' He got in front of her so she had to stop walking. 'What's worse, okay? What's worse for you? Not accepting the guitar and going home to the exact same problems that drove you away in the first place? Or turning a blind eye to the idea that possibly maybe perhaps it's been nicked, and using it to help you sort out whatever problems you've got?' He raised an eyebrow. Gave her a quick half-smile. 'Like I said. Up to you, yeah?'

She looked at the guitar. The feeling inside that it could solve so many of her problems was a powerful one. The thought that she could still maybe come out of this horrible situation smelling sweeter than she did right now was tugging at her. She wanted to believe him, really wanted to be convinced. And it was actually quite easy to let his wide grin and glittery blue eyes win.

She took the guitar from him. 'Thank you.'

'My pleasure,' he grinned. 'It's got a case too, you know.'

FIVE

She had the sun on her face. Almost – not quite, but Amy could *almost* forget where she was. This was the best she'd felt in ages. The best she'd felt since this whole sorry mess had started on that wrong train from Durham. She was still enough of a teenager to prickle at the thought of her mother ever being right, but she would always have to be grateful that she'd bullied her into going to her guitar lessons.

She gently broke off a chunk of chocolate, folded it up in her tongue and let it slowly melt. It was as warm in her mouth as the sun was on her closed eyelids.

Of course, her mother had really wanted her to learn the violin, or the piano, or (horror of horrors) the *flute*. Wanting to rebel even at an early age, Amy had insisted on the guitar, and then regretted it when she found out how much hard work was involved. But as she got older, playing had very probably become her greatest pleasure. She was good too – not wonderful, not the best, but pretty damn good. And the Gibson was a joy in her hands.

Only an hour earlier Amy had taken up a spot outside Woolworths as planned, standing in front of the 'Back 2 School' window display. She'd hoped it was a good sign that there were no other buskers on the high street, just a couple of young lads handing out leaflets to shoppers. She'd run through her repertoire of current pop in half an hour or so. But even then the shoppers on this busy Saturday afternoon had been generous, sprinkling the odd flashes of silver and spare copper onto the guitar's leather case at her feet. She hadn't been able to resist. She'd gathered up the coins excitedly: over £2 in half an hour. Although she knew she needed soap and clean knickers and proper food (and to phone her parents), she'd bought herself a bar of chocolate and was now sitting in the sunshine in the little park, loving the luxurious, sensual taste. The Gibson sat next to her.

Maybe chocolate is a girl's best friend. If not, then maybe it should be.

Bliss.

She chuckled at how much of a walking-tall cliché she was. Which was great, because when she woke this morning she quite honestly thought she might never smile again. And she knew it was thanks to the Can Man. If he hadn't first of all got hold of the Gibson for her, and then persuaded her to accept it, she'd be miserably hunched in the back of her father's car waiting for long-term captivity Durham-style. She would thank Canner properly the next time she saw him. Let him know how much she appreciated what he'd done. He'd turned out to be okay in the end, she decided.

She considered saving her last chunk of Galaxy. She rattled the coins in her pocket and felt sure she could spare enough for a second bar; she believed whole-heartedly she would soon raise more. It was certainly the right day to have picked: sunny Saturdays dragged everybody off the sofa. Savouring the last of her chocolate she decided she didn't want to play the same old naff pop songs all over again. The problem nowadays was that so few chart songs used the guitar as the main instrument any more. She was going to give the people of this grotty little town a slice of culture whether they liked it or not.

She returned to her spot (already she was thinking of it as *her* spot) outside Woolies. She was puffed-up with her re-found optimism, encouraged by the warm sun, and was doing her utmost to ignore the state of her clothes. She tried her best not to watch her fingers as she played. The black filthiness under her nails against the immaculate wood of the guitar took away some of the pleasure. She played the Allegro con spirito from the *Concierto de Aranjuez* by Joaquín Rodrigo. It was highly likely that nobody would be able to name the piece, but it was one of the best-known works of classical music for the guitar. If any, it was the one people might recognise from adverts, or from the movies.

It was an exciting piece to play, complicated enough to stretch her fingers and make them work hard. She could hear the rest of the orchestra in her head. Again passers-by sprinkled their spare change onto the guitar's case, but to Amy's surprise one or two of them actually took a few moments to stand and listen, straining under the weight of their shopping bags. They then left pound coins and fifty-pence pieces. Some people who were queuing for buses even walked across the road to listen, then had to run when their bus finally appeared. And most of them left money. She supposed it must seem odd: a tramp girl with greasy hair and filthy nails playing beautiful music. Certainly not something you saw every day of the week on the pavement outside Woolies.

One young woman stayed to listen to the whole piece. She was well dressed: expensive sunglasses, dark hair tied back from her neck in a loose plait. She made Amy feel uncomfortable because she looked like the kind of woman Amy had always imagined she would become when she was older. She'd always wanted to dress well, look sophisticated, turn heads . . .

Amy wished the woman would walk away – she wanted her to turn up her nose and stride away in distaste. Because that's exactly what Amy would do if the tables were turned. But she stayed until Amy finished playing.

Then she let a folded note drop onto the guitar case.

'Thank you,' she said. 'That was lovely. You play very well.' She smiled warmly before moving on.

Amy stared at the money, watched the woman cross the road, then had to look at the money again. She knelt down to check she wasn't seeing things. It was a £5 note. She scanned the street for the young woman but she'd melted away into the herds of shoppers. There was more than a twinge of embarrassment inside Amy – although from the way the woman had spoken to her, it hadn't sounded like pity. She'd said 'Thank you', so the money had been given because she'd enjoyed Amy's playing, and the music. Amy wrestled with the way that made her feel.

'I'm impressed!'

The voice made her jump. She looked up to see the Can Man standing over her, smiling his huge smile.

'Did you see that woman?' Amy asked, pointing the way she'd gone. 'She listened for ages, and she's given me this.' She waved the note.

'Nice woman.'

Amy nodded. She was counting quickly. 'I've got well over fifteen pounds!'

'That's excellent.'

Amy was stunned, but full of smiles.

'I liked what you were playing,' Canner said. 'Is it from a movie?'

She stood up slowly. 'Erm . . . not originally.' Her mind was elsewhere.

'I think I might have heard it in some cowboy movie when I was a kid.'

'Maybe,' Amy agreed. She was still looking at the heap of coins; because she was still so surprised she didn't quite know what to do with it.

'I like that type of music,' Canner was telling her. 'I'm getting a bit fed up of charty stuff.' Amy wasn't listening. 'All these pop songs nowadays with all that vocoder and effects and bleeping and blooping.' She was still staring, frowning at the money. 'It gets on my nerves. Just sounds like R2D2 having a wank, if you ask me.'

Now she looked at him. 'Excuse me?'

He grinned like a naughty boy. Then: 'I'd put it away if I were you,' he told her, nodding at the money. 'It's just my opinion, but I don't think buskers should look like they're making a profit.'

Amy nodded quickly and scooped the note and most of the coins into the side pocket of the case, zipping it up. 'Thanks.'

'No worries.' He fidgeted slightly. 'So, I better get moving. But maybe I'll see you later, yeah?'

'Yeah,' Amy said, running through her head what to spend her money on.

'Okay. See you, then.'

'Yeah. See you.' She was wondering how much more she could make.

'I'm a bit busy,' Canner told her. 'Or I'd hang around and listen some more.' Amy didn't actually hear him, she was too busy with her own thoughts, and he sloped slowly away.

Wow, she was thinking. This grotty little town must have been begging for some culture. She had so many classical pieces she could play, but few of them sounded quite so good without the backing of an orchestra. So she'd have to play the Rodrigo again – not that she minded if it was appreciated even half as much second time around.

She stood up and settled the guitar, but before she could play even the first note two young kids slid like snakes across the road towards her.

'Know anything decent?' the short one with the baseball cap asked. He had it pulled low over his spotty forehead. He was maybe nine, ten if he was lucky, runty-looking.

His mate was taller, wiry, but just as ugly. His T-shirt hung off his sharp shoulders like a sack. Maybe it was his big brother's. 'Know any Eminem?' He thought he was funny. Runty did too. They both laughed snottily.

'Run along, little boys,' Amy told them. 'Mummy needs you to kill the dog before she can cook it for your tea.'

The tall one squinted at her. 'Eh?'

Runty shrugged. 'You're a bit posh for a dosser, aren't you?'

'Just go away and bother someone else, will you?'

He shrugged again. The tall one kicked her guitar case, making it jingle with the coins inside. 'Loads of people've been giving you money, I've seen them. You've been raking it in. I reckon I'm gonna bring my guitar tomorrow. I'll make even more money.'

Amy simply stared at him.

Runty with the baseball cap shook his head quickly. 'Don't need to,' he told his mate. 'Just have hers.' And almost too quick to follow he struck out, snatching the leather case from the ground, and was away up the street as fast as his stumpy legs could carry him.

The tall one yelled in triumph and was quick on his mate's heels, shouting, 'Crusty bitch! Crusty bitch!' back at Amy.

For a second – two . . . three – she was too staggered by what had just happened right in front of her eyes to do anything. It was as if she had to drag the world into focus. She stood stock still and watched them run away laughing with the guitar case and her money. It was only when she saw Canner charging across the road, dodging cars and buses, that she was also able to give chase.

It wasn't easy running down the street with the Gibson. People kept getting in her way and the guitar kept bashing into them. They could see she was running, but instead of moving they stood to watch her approach, then swore as she barged past. She knocked one woman onto her backside and almost gored an old man with the head of the guitar as if it was a lance. She raced past Boots, dodged into the road to avoid the crush and ran along the double yellow lines.

She could see Canner ducking and weaving through the crowd up ahead. *Get them*, she willed him. *Catch the little bastards*.

He turned off the high street and darted down a side road. She ignored the faces of the shoppers as she followed, pushing back onto the pavement, narrowly avoiding piling into a post box. She'd never been the greatest of runners. She waved her arms too much.

As she rounded the corner into the narrow side road she could see a delivery lorry parked up at the back entrance to Superdrug. There were flattened cardboard boxes and plastic wrap littering the gutters on either side. Just behind the lorry Canner had Runty up against the red-brick wall, the Gibson's case at his feet. His tall pal was nowhere to be seen.

'Get off me!' Runty squealed, his face flushed red below the baseball cap's massive bill. 'Get off!'

Amy was out of breath, sweating, and just as red in the face. Canner saw her and shook the kid by the front of his T-shirt. 'Tell her you're sorry.'

'Piss off!'

He shook the kid harder. The cap fell off and underneath his hair was even greasier looking than Amy's. His fringe oozed forward over his spotty forehead.

'Get off or I'll get you done!'

Amy picked up the case and heard the coins rattle inside. She leaned in close to the ugly little upstart. 'I hope one day you meet someone twice as big as me who kicks you around like a football, just for laughs.'

'Get lost!'

She was amazed at his bravery, venomous even when he was pushed up against a wall by someone twice his size.

Canner shook him again, banged his head against the wall hard enough to warn him but not to seriously hurt. The kid yelped and squirmed. 'Even I wasn't quite such a nasty little shit as you when I was your age,' Canner told him.

'Get lost!' the kid replied.

'Do you want him?' Canner asked Amy.

Amy stepped up close to him and showed him her sharp, filthy nails. 'Maybe I should scratch my name in his face like I did with that other little boy yesterday. Or gouge his eyes out, maybe?' Runty squirmed and twisted, but couldn't get away from Canner. 'Leave him,' Amy decided. 'He's only a little runt, and the way he's going he'll not have chance to grow up enough to enjoy being a big one.'

Canner laughed and pushed the kid away forcefully, making him trip over his own feet. But he was back up on them quick enough, running away, yelling and swearing at them as he disappeared back onto the high street. 'You've gotta love them really, haven't you?' Canner said.

'If you say so,' Amy replied. Then: 'Thanks for that, Canner. I would never have got it back if you hadn't stopped him.'

'I didn't trust them the minute I saw them walking towards you. I spotted what they were up to straight away.' He shrugged. 'Takes one to know one, I suppose.'

'But I *do* mean thank you. For getting me the guitar in the first place, as well as for this.'

He smiled widely. They walked back towards the high street. Amy hoped he believed her. She couldn't explain that she wasn't used to saying thank you; it wouldn't sound right if she tried. She came from a family where you took what was offered because you could, not because it was a gift. She met his smile, and his sparkling blue eyes, and hoped that was enough to prove she meant what she said.

'So what are you going to do with your new-found wealth?' he asked.

'Soap and toothpaste!' she said brightly. '*Deodorant!*'

'Maybe you should celebrate, too.'

'What do you mean?'

'I could help you,' Canner said, his smile on full-beam. 'We could go out and get a meal in a nice restaurant somewhere. A bottle of wine, some—'

'I don't think I've got enough for that somehow . . .'

'So, I'll pay. My treat. To celebrate. You can tell me how wonderful I am, and how grateful you are that I'm around to save you all the time.' He winked. 'I like it when people are grateful.'

Something pinched in her head. She stopped walking and eyed him carefully. She watched his smile flicker uncertainly at the edges when he realised he was being scrutinised. Because maybe now it was adding up in her mind. Maybe now she was beginning to realise why the Can Man can, and does. She couldn't help but feel disappointed – then angry at herself for falling for one of the oldest tricks in the book.

'I don't mind paying,' he was saying, working particularly hard on his smile. 'I know a nice Italian place, kind of quiet – be a good way to get to know each other. Just the two of us. We could get a bit drunk and—'

'And maybe it would be my way of showing a little bit of appreciation for you getting me this wonderful, beautiful guitar. My way of saying thank you.'

He nodded, but it was an uncertain movement. His smile was fading fast: he'd heard the tone of her voice.

'It's like you do me a favour,' Amy said. 'And then I do you one back. Right? Do all the girls get to go for a nice Italian meal?' There was acid in her words. What a fool she was! 'Do they *all* show you a little bit of appreciation?' He'd fooled her all right. Fooled her good and proper. My God, she'd even said thank you and meant it!

His smile broke in two. 'No, I only—'

'Drop dead, Can Man!' she spat.

'What?'

His acting was good, spot-on in fact. Credit where it's due, she thought. But he was just like every other boy she'd ever met.

'I'm trying to—'

'You can have your guitar back,' she said. 'Shove it where it hurts most!' She thrust it out at him. He wouldn't take it, so she threw the leather case at him, spilling coins noisily across the pavement. Passers-by were staring – not that she cared. 'And you can have the money too for all I care! Just drop dead!' She strode away.

He grabbed her arm. She tried to shake him off, but he wouldn't let her. 'You've got the wrong end of the stick,' he said. 'I'm just—'

'*Let go of me!*' she hissed.

He dropped her arm as if it was on fire. 'Sorry, I didn't mean . . . Sorry. Honestly. I'm sorry.' He was backing away, and bumped into an old lady. 'Sorry,' he said to her quickly, then turned back to Amy. 'Sorry.' He hurried away across the road.

She watched him go. Her cheeks burned hot with her anger. She swept her greasy hair out of her eyes, and counted to ten to calm herself down. He had looked genuinely distraught but it was surely only because he'd been caught out in his slimy scheme. How dare he? *How dare he?* She wondered if Shelly knew about it. Probably. And that made her angrier still.

Her mother was right. Nobody in this world did anything for anyone unless they wanted something bigger in return.

Amy swept up as many of the dropped coins as she could.

There was a part of her that had been really warming to Canner. He'd seemed different. So different to the boys she knew from school. They were laddish, childish, vain yet so limp; dependent on Daddy's money and mostly very dull. Canner had come across as someone with a real sparkle inside him. His eyes dared you to take him seriously. Was he as flippant as he liked to pretend? You had to take the risk if you ever wanted to find out.

But his eyes had lied.

She was taken aback by how much this seemed to matter. She hadn't realised before that she'd wanted him to be different. She'd wanted his genuineness to be genuine. She'd wanted him to be as interesting and as complicated as he appeared. But he was just another boy whose balls were too full for him to be able to think straight.

She cursed him for making the money she'd earned feel tainted. She stuffed it into the pockets of her canvas jeans. They bulged. Well, he wasn't going to spoil her enjoyment of spending it, she assured herself. And she jangled off along the street towards Superdrug.

Soap, shampoo, huge tube of toothpaste and toothbrush. Not her usual deodorant – that was too expensive – but the least girlie scent she could find. She took her time looking: she was determined to enjoy herself again. Then from Woolworths knickers cheaper than any she'd ever dream of buying back home – but they were *clean*; two pairs. Two bars of chocolate, and a small but long-pondered-over bag of pick 'n' mix. It felt good counting out her change into the sales assistant's hand and holding up the rest of the queue. She wished Canner was here to watch her enjoying herself, thanks to him, but without having to pay him back in any way whatsoever. She wandered around a second-hand bookshop and bought a tatty copy of *The Beach* for 75p. Never having got round to seeing the movie, she fancied reading the book.

She had just under £6 left. (She should save some to call her parents.) She bought two apples, a banana, a still-warm baguette, some bottled water. The bus to the swimming baths cost her 75p, the entry ticket £2 and 50p to keep her guitar safe. She stood under the shower for half an hour before she even opened her shampoo and soap, simply enjoying the hot water. She then used three quarters of the shampoo and enough toothpaste to make her feel sick. She washed her dirty knickers. She wished she'd bought a razor to shave her legs – they were worse than a rugby player's.

In the changing room she wanted to sit in the cubicle in her new knickers as long as she could before putting her dirty jeans and T-shirt back on over her freshly scrubbed pink skin. But she knew she had to phone her parents.

She sat in the café overlooking the swimming pool and treated herself to a coffee. She just wanted to feel normal, civilised, for as long as she could before returning to the warehouse. There were lots of children in the pool, clambering on and off a huge green inflatable octopus with fat, sausage tentacles; squealing and splashing without a single solitary care in the world. She usually shied away from loud children, but even to her it looked like a lot of fun.

She sipped at her coffee slowly, letting it go cold because finishing it would mean she had to leave. She couldn't get over the hollow hurt Canner had caused inside her – and the embarrassed frustration she felt having fallen for his lies. Not that it should matter, she told herself. Why did she care? If she could earn £10 a day from busking she could have a train ticket home in next to no time.

With a sigh she decided she should leave. She had to phone her parents. Maybe she should call the thief too. No, it had to be her parents. She'd promised herself she would. She knew she had to. And she also knew how the conversation would go. In her head she ran through the emotions she was bound to feel, from contrition to shame to feeling petty and spoilt and childish. She pulled the faces she thought would suit each emotion best.

With a great force of will she drained her coffee and dug in her pocket for the change. But without realising it she'd spent most of her money. She had only coppers left. She told herself she felt suitably guilty.

And promised she'd call them tomorrow.

Six

When Amy got back to the warehouse she found Shelly still buried deep down inside her sleeping bag – which annoyed her at first. She'd wanted to spend the evening alone again, enjoying her chocolate and reading *The Beach*. It did strike her as kind of strange that Shelly was still here, however. Amy didn't have the faintest idea what her kip-mate got up to during the day, but she rarely reappeared until after it got dark.

So Amy made an effort to be extra noisy, hoping to wake her up and drive her out. But when Shelly's face emerged from the folds of the sleeping bag looking sickly pale, her eyes red and swollen, even Amy wasn't a big enough bitch not to feel a twinge of concern.

'Sorry, did I wake you?' she asked, cringing inside at her own hypocrisy, but hoping she at least sounded a little sincere.

Shelly forced a thin smile. 'No worries – it's about time I got up and found something to eat.' She raised herself up onto one elbow.

Amy sat down on her own mattress opposite. 'Are you okay?'

Shelly considered the question for what seemed like an eternity. Then: 'Not really,' was the honest answer. 'But it'll pass. Always does. Same old time-of-the-month feeling sorry for myself. Although it's not usually this bad.'

Amy had always been lucky – she'd never suffered particularly badly. She was a little tearful now and again, but she'd always had enough chocolate and moody CDs to help her cope. She watched as Shelly shuffled herself upright in her sleeping bag, exposing as little as possible of herself to the outside world. Being ill when you're away from home, or at least away from anyone who's ready to dish out the much-needed TLC, is one of the most miserable experiences.

Shelly swayed slightly, eyes closed, uncomfortable.

'Maybe this'll help.' Amy offered her one of the bars of chocolate she'd bought earlier. What does it matter? she thought. She should be able to buy another one tomorrow.

Shelly looked genuinely surprised. But she accepted with an honest-to-goodness smile. 'Just what the doctor ordered. Bloody fantastic. Thank you.'

'Can't you get anything from a doctor for the pain?' Amy asked.

'Used to. But it's not been so easy since I've been in here.'

Amy nodded to show she understood. 'Of course.' Then: 'Not as though they'd give you chocolate on prescription anyway.' She peeled the wrapper from her second bar and snapped off a chunk: 'Here's to real healing power,' she said, and popped it into her mouth.

They grinned at each other.

There was an opportunity here to make friends, for Amy to let down her shield, she knew that. Better than spending every night curled up on a lumpy mattress feeling sorry for herself. She'd decided to stay until she'd raised enough money to be able to make her own way home, and it would be good not to have to be alone in the meantime. But Amy had always found it hard to trust. She'd never been the most open person in the world, even with her friends from school. And she still felt as though she'd been burned by the Can Man.

'Have you known Canner long?' she asked Shelly.

Shelly was immediately intrigued. She sat up that tiny bit straighter. 'As long as I've been here. Why?'

'How well do you know him?' Amy asked, ignoring Shelly's own question.

Shelly was letting a square of chocolate melt on her tongue. She licked her lips and said: 'He's asked you, hasn't he? I bet he has.'

'He asked me on a date,' Amy admitted. 'He tried to make out it was to celebrate, for my sake, but I could see right through him.'

Either the chocolate or the gossip – perhaps both – but something seemed to have animated Shelly; perked her up a little. 'What did he say?'

'He wanted to go to an Italian restaurant.'

'Aren't you the lucky girl?' Shelly said with a slow wink.

'Am I?' Amy didn't think so. She'd been hoping that the news would be a big surprise to the other girl, but her ugly thoughts about Canner seemed to be justified. Shelly wasn't in the least bit surprised, just amused.

'And what did you say?'

'I told him where he could shove it.'

'No! You didn't!' Shelly actually clapped her hands with delight. 'That's brilliant. I wish I'd been there!'

'What else was I meant to say? I was so angry at him. And disappointed too, I suppose. I was beginning to kind of like him.'

Shelly raised an eyebrow. 'Tell me more.'

Amy was saying more than she wanted to anyway. So now she just shrugged.

'He's difficult not to like,' Shelly said. 'I would have gone with him in a second.' She snapped her fingers. 'Quick as that.'

Amy was confused. 'Honestly?'

Shelly popped another square of chocolate in her mouth. 'Oh, yes. No doubt about it.' Again she snapped her fingers. 'Like that.'

'But it's all kind of slimy, isn't it?'

'What is?'

'The way he uses girls. The way he tries to come across as some latter-day Robin Hood, but he's only doing it to get into your knickers.'

Shelly was laughing, but Amy couldn't see the funny side of it. 'Hasn't he ever tried to take you on one of his "dates"?'

Shelly was quick to shake her head. 'No! *I've* never been asked.'

Now Amy was really confused. 'Hasn't he ever given you his "Can you get it, yes I can" spiel? He sounds like a mutant Bob the Builder.'

'He says it all the time. He and Matty built this kip for me.'

'And he's never tried it on?' Amy couldn't help sounding disbelieving.

'Not even once. Worst luck.'

'But . . .'

Shelly leaned forward conspiratorially. 'Everybody knows he's got the hots for you. It's the best piece of gossip this place has had in weeks.'

Amy stayed quiet, not sure whether to feel embarrassed or not.

'He offered me a new sleeping bag if I asked you for him. But I told him that was the kind of thing you get your friend to do in the playground when you're six. Pete bet him a quid he wouldn't have the guts to ask you himself. And then another quid that you'd say no.'

Amy hid her thoughts by nibbling on the edge of her chocolate.

'Poor Canner,' Shelly was saying. 'We all told him you were far too posh for him.'

'What?' Amy didn't like the sound of that.

'He's not your type, surely. I'm guessing you go for doctors' sons. Or estate agents. Cars, suits and money money money are a posh bird's biggest turn-on, aren't they? And I can't say I blame you, either. But you've got to feel sorry for Canner if he at least plucked up the courage to try.'

'My father's an estate agent.'

Shelly obviously thought this was one of the funniest things she'd ever heard. She laughed so loud that her face creased in pain and she had to suck in sharp breaths, her body reminding her how rough it felt.

Amy, however, suddenly felt alone all over again: she now realised what impression of herself she'd given to these people. She knew it was her fault – she'd made a point of wanting to keep her distance. She'd thrown up her shield without a second thought, locked down the barriers and acted like the high and mighty bitch queen from hell. In short, just like her mother.

So there were two reasons for what she did next. The first was to prove everyone wrong. She wasn't going to have anybody – *anybody* – thinking they knew what kind of a person she was. She refused to be that simple to pin down and examine.

And the second reason?

Well, maybe there was a part of her that was intrigued by the Can Man. Maybe she'd been right when she thought there was something in him worth searching out.

She fished out her bag of carefully chosen pick 'n' mix and plonked the bag down between herself and Shelly. 'Tell me about him, then,' she said. 'All the juicy bits, don't leave anything out.'

Shelly looked like she might explode with delight. 'Are you serious? You're not telling me you're actually interested, are you?'

Amy smiled coyly. She'd thought of a third reason. She realised Canner must like her for real if she was the only girl he'd ever invited out, and she certainly never shied away from compliments. Then a fourth one jumped to mind: her mother would hate him. And a fifth: she thought he had beautiful eyes.

So, there were lots of reasons to accept his invitation when she thought about it.

SEVEN

Amy's father believed in paying for the best, and the best came at a price. This was his philosophy, from cars to eau-de-Cologne to restaurants. If it was expensive, it had to be the best. Obviously. Canner's choice of restaurant would not have matched her father's. It was along some scruffy side street, barely distinguishable from the fish-and-chip shop or the building society. Inside it was cramped and the lighting was dingy, not dimmed. There were not-quite-fresh flowers in the middle of the table. The paintings of vineyards and maps of Italy on the walls were well over the top in Amy's opinion. The waiters, with their bad accents, were probably from Doncaster. Amy was beginning to wonder if she would live to regret this.

Canner was enjoying himself, however. He'd been chatty in the car, and now seemed eager to have a good time. 'Let's get a bottle of wine. What d'you fancy?'

Amy didn't even bother to read the list – she just picked the name of one of the most expensive and watched for his reaction. It was a little spiteful perhaps, but she wanted to see how flash he actually believed he was.

'Is it nice?' he asked, without batting an eye.

She didn't have the foggiest, but nodded all the same. He'd passed the first test anyway.

After her talk with Shelly last night (which told her nothing more about Canner because nobody knew anything about him anyway, not even his real name) she'd passed the word around the people sitting amongst the lights in the centre that she wanted to see him. And then when he'd appeared she'd accepted his invitation. He'd been surprised, but had done his best to appear nonchalant. They'd arranged times and parted; her back into the kip, him over to his friends in the centre. Both she and Shelly had rolled their eyes and giggled at the crescendo of cat-calls and wolf-whistles which had filled the warehouse.

Today she'd spent her time busking again, although she'd been nowhere near as successful as she had yesterday. She told herself it was because it was a Sunday – less people out and about; fewer shops open too. Which was perfectly true, but only managing £6.78 all day worried her. It was going to take a lot longer to raise the money to get home if that was all she could expect on a normal day.

Most of it had already gone now: sandwich for lunch, another shower at the swimming pool (but no phone call home). She'd also borrowed some of Shelly's clothes and taken her own T-shirt and jeans to the launderette. The jeans had come out all right, but her T-shirt was stretched so shapeless now that nothing would save it. Tonight she was wearing one of Shelly's. It was red, with the words MY LIFE in bold white lettering across the chest. On Shelly the statement probably looked like a rather subdued comment of teen angst, whereas thanks to Amy's ample bosom it was more like the last deranged cry of a kamikaze pilot.

Canner had done his best to smarten up too. Shirt and trousers, and even a shave. He didn't dress as well as the boys back home; he was so very different to them, but wasn't that what attracted her to him? She hated vanity in men – boys who wore more perfume than she did, who couldn't walk past mirrors without staring in them. Canner was, without question, rough around the edges. Which was fine. It was whatever was on the inside that had made her want to be here tonight.

And if things developed she could help mould the outside anyway, couldn't she?

When the wine arrived he ordered some garlic bread. They decided to share the largest Four Seasons pizza the waiter could carry.

They sat in silence with the expensive wine.

They'd already talked about their respective days in the car, and had chatted politely about the restaurant and the menu when they arrived. Now they were sitting waiting for the food and had to find some other topic of polite conversation. But that wasn't Amy's way.

She took a sip of her wine (which wasn't great considering the price) and asked: 'What's your real name?' She was pleased to see the shocked look in his eyes.

He took a sip of his wine to fill the silent beat. 'Secret,' he said.

'No, come on, I want to know. Seriously, what is it?'

'Warehouse etiquette,' he told her. 'No awkward questions, remember?'

The garlic bread arrived, and she could see him heave a sigh of relief. He was probably expecting her to stuff her mouth too full to ask him again. She decided to let him off this time. But he'd have to learn she didn't give up easily.

'It's good,' he said, swallowing a large mouthful.

To her surprise, she agreed. It was freshly baked and wonderful.

'What made you change your mind?' he asked. 'About coming tonight?'

'I made a mistake,' she admitted. Then, when she saw the stricken look on his face: 'No,' she said quickly. 'Not now; back then. Saying no was the mistake.' He looked happier. 'I wasn't sure why you invited me. I thought you were expecting me to swoon at your feet with gratitude for getting me the guitar.'

'It would have been nice,' he said. 'It's not often I meet a girl who doesn't. Most are very grateful indeed.'

She narrowed her eyes at him until he smiled. She realised he was toying with her as much as she was with him. He chewed nonchalantly on his garlic bread, sipped at his wine. And if it was a battle of wills he was after, she thought to herself, then he was about to meet his match.

'I didn't know you had a boss,' she said.

He paused with his garlic bread halfway to his mouth. 'Boss? What d'you mean? I don't have a boss.'

'Shelly said someone called Lem runs the warehouse. And that you're just his lackey.' These hadn't been Shelly's words at all, but Canner wasn't to know that.

He laughed, shaking his head. 'No, we're good mates. He just—'

'Shelly told me he's the one who says what goes in the warehouse. People call him King of Crap Palace.'

'Well, yeah. He's the one who decided on the rule, and he—'

'So if he runs the warehouse, he must be your boss.' She took a drink of her wine. 'It must be tough having your "good mate" tell you what to do all the time.'

He shook his head again. 'No, you don't understand . . .'

'No, I don't. Because if this Lem runs the warehouse, then . . .'

'If you'd just let me explain . . .'

She folded her arms. 'Go on, then.'

'I am *trying*.'

'You're not doing a very good job of it.'

He stared hard at her. 'Are you purposely trying to wind me up?'

She shrugged. 'Maybe.' Another quick sip of wine. 'What's your real name?'

He held his head in hands. 'Bloody hell!' he wailed. 'Let's

hope the pizza turns up before the men in white coats come to take me away. I'd hate to be driven insane on an empty stomach.'

She smiled sweetly. 'Sorry.' While in her head she congratulated herself: fifteen–love.

The pizza arrived, and it was even better than the garlic bread. She couldn't understand why the restaurant itself looked so terrible, when the food they served was this good. Back home she would have turned up her nose at this place. Her father would have walked by without a second glance. More fool him, she thought.

'Good, yeah?' Canner mumbled through a mouthful, watching her closely.

'Very,' she agreed, and saw how pleased her comment made him. Ah well, she told herself. Fifteen all. She met his blue eyes and smiled.

They'd reached that point where they didn't need to think about the conversation any more; there was no struggle to fill the breaks and lulls. They chatted away quite happily, polishing off the pizza and the bottle of wine in next to no time. Amy wasn't sure what it was exactly – undoubtedly the wine; perhaps being full for the first time in days – but she was feeling quite dizzy in a pleasant kind of way. She felt as though she had delicate silvery bubbles floating around inside her head. She leaned back in her chair and patted her porky-round belly.

Canner swallowed the last of his pizza almost regretfully, but gave a big, contented grin. 'Everything okay?' he asked.

'Yes. Yes, definitely.' She nodded quickly, popping those silvery bubbles. 'You look happy.'

'It was delicious.'

She couldn't stop staring at him.

'What's up?'

'Did you know that when you smile like that you look like Fozzie Bear?'

He stopped smiling sharpish.

'No, no.' She waved a hand to reassure him. 'I've always thought the Muppets were really cute. And Fozzie's my favourite. Absolutely.'

He smiled widely again. He picked up the empty bottle of wine. 'So let's get this straight,' he said. 'It only takes one bottle to make you say I'm cute, which by my calculations means that after two you'll start to believe I'm handsome. So it should only take three to get you thinking I'm sexy. And after four you'll be as randy as a goat!'

She squealed with indignation and kicked him under the table.

'Waiter,' he called. 'Another bottle, please. Quick as you like.'

She went to kick him again, but stopped herself. What on earth did she think she was doing? Look at the way she was acting! She might be a little tipsy, but that was no excuse for being such a *girl*. She saw Canner grinning from ear to ear, and that devil-may-care sparkle in his eyes. And all she could think was: fifteen–thirty to him.

So when the fresh bottle of wine appeared she refused to let him fill her glass. 'Only if you tell me your real name,' she said.

He rolled his eyes. 'Back on this, are we? You wouldn't believe me if I told you.'

'Try me.'

'You'll laugh.'

'Probably. If it's embarrassing, then definitely.'

He sighed deeply. He wasn't happy about revealing it. But, 'Robin,' he admitted.

Amy almost dropped her glass. '*Robin!*'

'Shush!' He scowled at her and went red from the tip of his nose to the point of his chin.

'You really *are* Robin Hood!'

'Robin Radcliffe, actually.'

Amy laughed so hard she thought she might wet herself.

Canner, the Can Man, *Robin Radcliffe*, looked down at his glass, running his fingers uncomfortably up and down the stem, and hunched himself up, shrinking with embarrassment. She didn't class this as a victory, however. She refused to – that wouldn't be fair. It was more like a privilege, wasn't it, to be trusted with his secret?

'I prefer Canner,' she told him, and poured herself some wine.

'Thank God for that.'

They drank their second bottle of wine slowly.

Amy ran her finger round the rim of her glass. 'You know, you rescued me yesterday.'

'Did I? How come?'

'By persuading me to take the guitar. I wasn't lying when I said I was planning to go home. I was going to phone my parents to tell them to come and fetch me. I'd nearly given up on myself, and was going to sit back and let Mummy and Daddy do with me exactly as they wished. I was going to be a good girl. And you've kept me bad.' She smiled at him. It was a tiny bit lopsided because of the wine, but hey, nobody's perfect.

'I know exactly what they'll say when I tell them I've been robbed,' she continued. 'But at least I haven't gone running to them for help. I wish I could just get my things back, and pretend it never happened. I've asked him, but he's such a—'

'What do you mean, you've asked him? D'you mean the bloke that stole your stuff?'

She nodded. 'He's got my mobile and I call him up. That's where any money that I had left went – on begging him.'

Canner was thoughtful. 'Give me your mobile number when we get back,' he said.

'Why?'

'*I* want to talk to him.'

'Do you think you can get him to give me my things back?'

He wanted to say, 'Of *course* I can.' She saw his face move – his lips even began to form the words, because that was what he always said. But even the Can Man was going to find this particular request difficult.

'I can try,' he said eventually.

'That's good enough for me,' she told him. 'It would be wonderful not to go running back to Durham with my tail between my legs.'

'Are your parents really that bad?'

She was ready to say yes, and it almost slipped out. But she remembered who she was talking to, and that most of the people in the warehouse, most of Canner's friends, didn't have anything like the luxury of choice she did. 'I suppose not, no. Just domineering, self-righteous, condescending, irritating, and a pain in the backside.'

'Like most people's, then.'

'Hmm.' She didn't want him to think she was some kind of fraud. She stared down at the wine in her glass.

'And it seems like a lot of hassle you're going to, just to punish them.'

'I know I'm not exactly hard up like most people in the warehouse. I know I'm not . . .'

'The warehouse is for anybody who needs it.'

'Is it wrong to want to do your own thing, and to be your own person? My parents seem to think they've got my life all mapped out for me, but it feels as if both of them are using a different compass. Dad wants me to work for him at the estate agent's – that's all I need in his eyes. He'll sort me out, he'll make sure his little girl's hunky-dory and A-okay. But how can you be your own person when Daddy's the boss?'

'Worse than having your best mate as the boss, I reckon.' He gave her a sly wink.

She pouted back. 'And Mum. She wants me to go to uni, not because I need to, but because that's what everybody does nowadays, isn't it? And we'd hate to be the odd ones out, wouldn't we? But I'd only go to Durham Uni, because it's close enough to keep the leash on. And it doesn't matter too much if I get my degree at the end of the three years, because university is where you meet the nice doctors' sons, and the lawyers-to-be. Someone whose kids I should decide I'm desperate to have. If I play my cards right, I'll never have to work and can join my mother's coffee mornings, where she'll be able to show off the grandchildren, because won't she be such a young-looking grandmother?'

'Easy life, though,' Canner said.

'Crap life.'

He pointed at her T-shirt. 'Your life.'

'My life,' she agreed.

They chinked glasses.

Very few people know how to listen, but Amy noticed that when she talked, Canner listened without distraction to what she said, and only to what she said. She found that important. Something else that marked him out from the crowd of boys back home.

'So if I go back now I'll be bundled up into it all,' she said. 'But by staying here and going back on my own terms I kind of prove my point, and make my stand, no matter how petty it seems. You never know, I may even gain a smidgen of independence.'

Canner lifted his glass. '"God grant me the serenity to accept the things I cannot change, courage to change the things I can and wisdom to know the difference."'

'What's that?'

'It's called the Serenity Prayer. My dad was an alky and he

used to say it all the time. I think they taught him it at those Alcoholics Anonymous meetings.'

'*Was* an alcoholic? Does that mean he's okay now?'

'Not really.'

Amy nodded, just to show she understood not to ask any more, then lifted up her glass to chink once again with his. 'Still sounds like good advice to me.'

'I always thought so.'

He sat up straight, as if physically pulling himself together. 'Listen,' he said, looking around the restaurant, 'I think we'd better make a move, yeah? I don't want to be the last table here.' Only two other tables were still occupied. 'This is the plan.' He leaned forward across the table and whispered, 'You go to the toilet, and climb out the window. I checked it earlier from the alley outside – hopefully it's still open. I pulled a wheelie bin underneath for you to climb onto. While you're gone, I'll—' The look of abject horror on Amy's face stopped him. He reflected her look with one of surprise. 'What's wrong?' he asked, all innocence and light.

She couldn't believe what he was saying. 'You're planning on not paying, aren't you?'

He scoffed. 'Do you think I can afford these prices?'

'Oh my God!' She stared at him open-mouthed. No wonder he'd let her choose the most expensive wine. Game, set and match to him, she thought.

'Shhh!' He checked over his shoulder furtively. 'It'll be fine. You go out the toilet window, I'll leg it out the door. They'll chase me; you'll be fine. We'll meet back at the car. You remember where we parked, don't you?'

'I don't believe this!'

'Keep your voice down,' he hissed.

'Have you got no money whatsoever?'

'Have you?'

'Oh my God!' She felt extremely sober all of a sudden.

'It'll be fine.'

'If I didn't like you so much, I'd kill you.'

He brightened. 'You like me?'

She narrowed her eyes at him. The problem was, she honestly did.

'How much?' He leaned closer, grinning his huge grin.

'Enough to risk my neck climbing out of a toilet window for you.'

'That much, eh?' He sounded particularly smug.

'Look,' she said, draining her glass. 'Let's do this now, because if I start to think about it for even a second longer I'll realise what a completely stupid and moronic thing it is I'm about to do, and then won't do it at all.' She asked a passing waiter the way to the ladies' and strode away without looking back.

It was dank and cold in the toilet – chipped tiles on the wall and an empty paper-towel dispenser; two cubicles and only one basin. She closed the door behind her. She really wanted a pee, but decided the need to get out through the window was greater. To reach it she was going to have to climb onto the basin. And it wasn't the biggest window in the world either. She had horrible images in her mind's eye of getting stuck halfway, her boobs and hips just too big to slide through.

She stared at herself in the mirror. What on earth was she doing here? She was so scared someone would catch her and drag her back by her ankles. She cursed the name Robin Radcliffe. She couldn't believe she was actually going through with this. 'What am I *doing*?' she asked her reflection.

She checked the two cubicles to make sure they were empty, then took a deep breath before she clambered up onto the wet and slippery basin. Oh my God. Oh my *God*. She heaved and pulled her top half through the window, puffing and gasping with the exertion, feeling her belly groan with half a Four Seasons. She just wasn't built for this kind of thing.

She got her top half through, out into the fresh night air of the alleyway, but she wasn't sure how she was going to get the rest of her to follow. She simply flopped there, half in, half out, wagging her legs up and down, pointlessly jerking her arms in front of her. Just imagine if Mum could see her now. She'd have a heart attack. No, she'd go grey first. Then have kittens, then climb the walls, then hit the roof. And *then* have a heart attack.

It was this thought, no doubt topped off with the wine, that suddenly gave her the giggles as she flopped across the windowsill like a seal on the beach. 'Does my bum look big in this?' She shook with silent giggles.

Only when she heard voices back in the restaurant did panic help her to wiggle and shuffle herself free. She tumbled unceremoniously and painfully into the alleyway, landing on the wheelie bin which skittered out from underneath her. Bruised and winded, she picked herself up and ran as if her life depended on it.

She took a couple of wrong turns, continually checking over her shoulder, scared she was being followed, and thought she was lost. At last she found the right street and the car.

Canner was already sitting inside. 'What took you so long?'

She was panting badly. The Four Seasons and the wine settled in her belly like the load in a slow washing machine. She refused to speak to him and climbed into the passenger seat, slamming the door closed after her.

'Aren't you talking to me? Didn't you enjoy the pizza?'

She answered by not answering. Make him work at his apology, she thought. There was a scrap of paper on the seat and she snatched it up from underneath her. She was going to crumple it up and toss it out the window, but the word 'receipt' caught her eye. Then she saw the name of the restaurant printed at the top. 'This is a receipt.'

He nodded.

'You paid.'

He nodded again.

'You *paid*!'

'I wanted to know if you'd really go through with it,' he said matter-of-factly. 'I'm impressed.' He grinned at her and patted her on the arm. 'Well done you.'

She punched him in the face hard enough to blacken his eye.

EIGHT

The streets were quiet. They walked back to the warehouse, deciding to leave the car where it was because Canner didn't want to drive after having more than his fill of wine. He'd pick it up again in the morning. It was a warm night and Amy didn't mind walking. He made her laugh; it hadn't taken her long to see the funny side. They were both drunk. And he laughed hard enough to bring tears to his eyes when she told him how she'd got stuck halfway through the window. He reached out to hold her hand and she didn't stop him. She was enjoying the walk, enjoying his company. He complained about how badly his eye was hurting. She kissed it better. He lifted his head to kiss her lips and she didn't stop him.

There was what sounded like a party going on when they finally made it back to the warehouse. Apparently someone had appeared with several bottles of cheap red wine and there was a large group sharing it in the centre. Shelly was there too, obviously feeling much better than the day before. Canner said he couldn't face any more alcohol, so they went to Amy's kip, and had it all to themselves.

It felt good. She let him undress her. She was drunk and had to hold back the giggles at first. What if they got caught? What if someone could hear? It was dark but she wanted to be able to see his eyes. His smile was fuzzy at the edges with drink, his words a little slurred, but he was confident with his hands and with his kisses. He told her she was beautiful. He made her feel beautiful. She felt like the centre of the universe. And it felt good. So good. His kisses were so warm.

She stretched out beneath him. She was drunk. She closed her eyes and could have been floating. He held her close. She was the one and only girl in the whole world to ever feel this way. She let herself go. And when he was inside her he said: 'I think I love you.' She kissed him. 'I think I love you too,' she said. Because of the moment.

When they curled up together to sleep she felt him slow his breathing to match hers.

Shelly disturbed them in the morning. She stumbled into the kip to find them still in each other's arms. 'Don't mind me,' she said loudly, and collapsed onto her own mattress with a huge woof of a sigh. 'And I don't need all those thank-yous just because I stayed out of your way last night, even though I know you're desperate to give them to me.' She sounded as though she was still drunk herself.

Neither Canner nor Amy answered. Amy didn't even want to open her eyes just yet.

'I take it you *did* have a good time last night, then?'

Canner stretched and yawned and ran his hands through his hair. 'Don't start,' he warned. Then: 'What time is it?'

'Time you sorted out that new lad. What's his name? Robbie? I've never seen so much puke.'

Canner groaned. 'What've you done to him, Shelly?'

'Don't blame me. Nothing to do with me.' She rolled herself up into her sleeping bag, still fully clothed.

Canner turned over to face Amy. She was keeping her eyes closed against her hangover headache. It wasn't as bad as some she'd experienced, but this one came with more consequences. There was a needle prickling somewhere inside her which was nothing to do with the drink. It was prickling at another part of her head altogether. She kept her eyes closed in an effort to ignore it.

'I'd better go,' Canner told her, brushing her hair from her cheek.

She nodded slowly and made a small, sleepy noise of agreement.

'You're okay, yeah?'

She kept her eyes closed as she smiled. 'Yeah. Just, you know . . .' She wanted him to go.

He moved to kiss her, but she shied away.

'Urrgh! Garlic breath,' she told him. And it was half the truth. But she didn't want him kissing her in front of Shelly either. She reached out and squeezed his hand instead.

He laughed lightly. If he was disappointed he hid it well. 'I'll see you later,' he said. He pulled on his boxers and jeans underneath the blanket. 'Where abouts is Robbie, then?' he asked Shelly.

'How should I know?'

'Well, where did you leave him?'

'How should I know?'

Canner sighed and ducked out underneath the curtain.

Amy had her back to Shelly. Memories from last night were settling back in her head. The needle in her mind jabbed at her. She could see herself drunk, giggling, girly. She had been so easy for him.

'So?'

She pretended not to have heard, but Shelly shuffled closer in her sleeping bag.

'Sooo? What happened in here last night then, eh? Come on, girlfriend. Spill it!'

'Warehouse etiquette,' Amy replied without turning around, trying to sound light, hoping she sounded normal. 'No awkward questions.'

Shelly snorted through her nose. She shuffled back again. She was quiet for almost a whole minute before asking: 'Aren't you even going to tell me if he's got a big one?'

'*Per-lease!*'

Shelly took the hint and buried herself deep down in her

sleeping bag, as was her habit. It wasn't long before Amy heard muffled snores.

What Amy needed was a can of Irn Bru. She hated the stuff usually – it made her teeth ache with its sweetness – yet it was the best cure for a hangover she'd ever come across. A can in the morning and she could even dupe her mother into believing the night before had been spent revising, not sprawled on Juliet's floor with a bottle of vodka and a carton of orange juice. Adam Price had introduced her to Irn Bru's almost magical healing properties one morning after an impromptu party at his parents' summer house last year. It had been the morning after she'd lost her virginity to his older brother, Jeremy.

All the girls wanted to catch Jeremy Price. He'd paid her a lot of attention that night, flattered her in front of the others. Upstairs in his parents' bedroom she'd been able to taste the gin on his lips, but she hadn't been drinking, not then. Afterwards he'd left her on the over-soft mattress which smelled of lavender with her jeans and knickers still around one ankle. He'd been the Big Man of the party with his friends downstairs. When she stopped crying she'd got too drunk to care.

Canner was her second, and she'd been just as easy for him. And she'd told him she loved him. But it wasn't true. It couldn't be true. He'd said it first; she'd followed. It was the wine that had made her say it. As well as the whole night together, and yet also the single split second of time.

But it had been so different to Jeremy Price, hadn't it? Canner was so different.

She went taut like one of her guitar strings when she heard footsteps outside the kip. The Can Man poked his head under the curtain. 'He's dead to the world. You must have really wiped him out, Shelly . . .' He stopped when neither of the girls moved.

Amy could feel him watching her. Please let him think I'm sleeping. Please don't try to wake me. She could sense he was tempted to curl up on the mattress next to her again. He hovered, wanting to be with her again, no doubt wanting to have sex again; to prove himself one more time. Shelly's snores must have convinced him they were both asleep, however, and at last he retreated quietly.

To get some more sleep would have been wonderful, but the needle in Amy's head was not going to let her. She dressed quickly, quietly so as not to disturb Shelly and have to face more questions. She felt like a thief sneaking out of the warehouse. She took the guitar and hurried downstairs. It wasn't just Canner she was avoiding, but everyone, because of course everyone would know.

She was so confused. Maybe he'd lied too. Maybe he'd been caught up in the moment too. But she wanted him to have meant it, even when she was telling herself that *she* hadn't. Could you fall in love so quickly? Was it possible? Surely not. How was she to know anyway?

She'd found him so attractive because he was different. Yet wasn't that difference what was stopping her now? She thought so; yes. She could just imagine the look on her friends' faces. But why should it matter? Because that's what she'd been taught.

It was a brisk, windy day. No sun today. She tried busking. She couldn't really relax and enjoy it. Playing the guitar was usually her best escape. This guitar, however, was what had started it all.

Her head felt too full, and was in desperate need of emptying, or at least sorting. After a painful hour and a half and only £1.16 she gave up and went to sit in the park.

Canner was stronger and more independent inside than she could ever pretend to be. He'd most likely laugh at her when he found out what a pampered pet she really was. He'd probably run a mile anyway, so what was she worried about? It was just that she'd never felt like she had last night: in the restaurant, walking back to the warehouse, or alone together in the kip. She'd never met anyone like him before.

And now she was thinking in clichés. She couldn't sit still, so she walked the streets.

She'd told him she loved him on the spur of the moment because she was drunk. She didn't want to hurt him – she liked him so much, more than anyone she'd ever met before – but she'd only just met him so she couldn't really love him, could she?

Maybe he felt the same. Maybe he'd been caught in the moment too.

But it would hurt if he'd lied to her.

And now she was just thinking in circles.

She walked from what seemed like one end of the town to the other, and back again. She got herself lost on purpose, then was surprised when she came across a street she recognised. She walked off her hangover, but couldn't get rid of her heavy thoughts.

She'd walked past several telephone boxes, ignoring every single one. Now, however, she needed to talk to somebody who might listen. There was a phone box on the corner outside an empty primary school, closed for the holidays. She thought about it for only a second before stepping inside and fishing in her pockets for the money she'd made earlier. She had to dig around in the copper to find the few ten- and twenty-pence pieces. She was going to phone her parents.

She dialled the code, the first four digits – then swore at herself for her cowardice as she hung up. She called her mobile instead and listened to it ring. The thief didn't answer but she didn't leave a message, wanting to keep as much of her money as she could. She was about to leave when she stopped herself. She leaned her forehead against the glass. With a sigh like a condemned prisoner who's finally come to terms with the inevitable, she dug in her pocket for her change again. She picked up the receiver and deposited the coins. This time she dialled 141 first, then she phoned home. It rang twice.

'Ian O'Connor speaking.'

She was so tempted to slam the receiver down and run, but . . . 'It's me.'

'Amy? Amy! Thank God! Where are you, darling? Where are you? Are you all right, sweetheart?'

'Yes. I'm fine, Dad. Honestly. I'm fine.'

'Louisa. Louisa! It's Amy! Tell me where you are, darling. We've been worried sick.'

'I'm fine, Dad. I'm just—'

And then her mother got hold of the phone. 'Come home now.'

'Mum, I'm—'

'We've called the police and your grandmother. You've got everybody worried sick. So you've made your point, darling. Well done. Now come home.'

'Don't you even want to know where I am?'

'Wherever you are they must have an airport close by. Your father will give you his credit card details – just get yourself on the first plane home. You've got everybody worried.'

'I'm in Outer Mongolia.'

'Please don't be obstinate, darling. Your grandmother's very ill. The worry's keeping her up at night. None of us can sleep. Come home now.'

She heard her father asking in the background if she was okay, but her mother was ignoring him.

'Phone to tell me what time you land and I'll come and meet you at the airport.'

'I'm having the best time ever.'

'Well I'm sorry, but now it's time to come home. You've got to get ready for university. You've got . . .'

'Mum, I . . .'

'. . . your father worried about the type of people you're meeting.'

'Mum, listen to me—'

'Who's that boy you're with?' she asked. 'Why does he keep answering your phone?'

'He's my boyfriend,' Amy said, and gently replaced the receiver.

Nine

This was the biggest gamble of all, wasn't it? No shield, no barriers. For the first time ever she was going to let somebody in – if that's what he wanted.

Canner was waiting for her when she got back to the warehouse; in the kip talking with Shelly, who was still wrapped up in her sleeping bag and looking worse than when the illness hadn't been self-inflicted.

'Please tell me you bought some more chocolate today,' she whined pitifully.

Amy showed her empty jeans pockets.

'I think I might die,' Shelly groaned, closing her eyes and slumping over onto her side as if to prove it.

'You okay?' Canner asked Amy. 'I've been looking for you, but you weren't busking in your usual spot. I really need you to give me your mobile number. I've tried getting in touch with a few people I know, but nobody's heard a thing.'

She nodded. 'I appreciate you trying.'

He shrugged. She suspected he believed the same as her, just wasn't willing to admit it yet. But it looked like her rucksack was long gone.

'So where've you been?' he asked.

'I've been walking. And thinking.'

'Yeah?' He sounded light, but looked uneasy. 'What about?'

Amy glanced at Shelly, whose eyes were closed, but whose radar ears were probably wide open. 'Let's go outside,' she said.

They walked along the quayside, the silence between them more awkward than it had ever been before. Amy knew Canner wasn't going to say a single word unless forced, so she made the first move. 'About what you said last night.'

Canner licked his lips, looked at his feet. 'Right.'

'I want to know whether you meant it or not.' She wanted him on the spot, his back against the wall, with nowhere to run. If what he'd said to her was true, and not just horny boy-talk, then he shouldn't be worried about admitting it again. She wasn't willing to gamble unless the odds were stacked in her favour.

'I said a lot of things,' Canner told her, trying on his smile. It didn't seem to fit quite as well as it had done last night. 'We were both a bit drunk. I can't remember everything. But I'm sure I meant most of them.'

'Try harder,' she told him. She nearly added, 'Prove to me you truly are different, that you think I really am special.' But she didn't want to put words out in the open that could simply be nodded and grinned at.

He took a big breath, held it. When he slowly released it he nodded. 'I didn't lie to you,' he said. 'I'm just a bit confused. It's all been a bit quick. I've never said it before. I—'

'Said what?' she asked.

'You said it too,' he told her. 'Did *you* mean it?'

She'd known all along he'd eventually get around to asking her this. 'I don't know,' she admitted. 'I was caught up in what was happening, in the whole night. I had a wonderful night. You made me feel special. I said it because it seemed right at the time. I don't know if I meant it.'

Canner had lost his wrestle with the smile. He was staring at his feet again. 'So what does it matter if *I* meant it or not?'

'Because then I can find out how truthful I was being. I've never met anyone like you before – you seem to be from a whole different world to me. I'm scared we might not be able to meet up in the middle. But if you meant what you said, then we can at least try, can't we?'

He blinked slowly. 'I meant it,' he told her.

'You meant what? What was it you said?'

'I think I love you.'

And the second time around it sounded even better.

So now Amy was in uncharted territory, and still without her rucksack or her guide book. She knew some people would wink knowingly and call it 'Fate', but she'd always hated the idea of not having a say in what was happening in her life, and to her those people were probably fools. She'd made up her mind not to think about it too hard. She'd fallen for Canner because of some quality in him that she hadn't been able to explain; it was just him, so why mess her head up trying to figure out what it was.

And vice versa. She didn't have a clue what he found so attractive about her (maybe he liked hard work) – she was just happy he did.

Ten

A typical summer's afternoon: rain. Amy wandered around Woolworths for the umpteenth time, browsing the same shelves of tat she'd browsed an hour before. Her gaze kept returning to the window in case it had stopped, or was easing, and she was a little more disheartened each time when it hadn't. She'd had a successful day busking (in *some* ways) and hadn't wanted to give up. She supposed she was now facing a long, soggy walk back to the warehouse. She hoped the Gibson's case was waterproof.

Shelly had protested yesterday about having to spend the second night in a row cast out of her kip. Amy had promised her some more chocolate. Shelly had insisted on a king-size Kit-Kat Chunky. Canner had gone out with Lem, Kinard and the new boy to fetch some more lights, but when he returned he was tense and angry, although he'd refused to explain why. It had taken Amy a long time to calm him down, and then they'd been able to talk. They'd lain next to each other, comfortable in the darkness, and had talked long into the night about anything and everything. The only taboo subject seemed to be Durham. Neither of them broached the question of her having to go home. It wasn't even a question, really. They both knew she had to, but neither had been willing to ask what would happen. They didn't want to look that far ahead. Being together was about forgetting the rest of the world's worries.

Unfortunately Amy now had her pockets full of change again, over £10 worth. The more she earned towards her ticket, the quicker the time to leave approached. That's why it had only been a successful day's busking in *some* ways.

She still didn't know if she was doing right. She was just feeling her way.

She checked the clock at the front of the store: 5.20. They'd be closing soon – time she was heading back. With a sly smile she bought two king-size Kit-Kat Chunkies. Who knew if an extra bribe might be needed tonight? She considered paying a fiver for a thin cagoule, then changed her mind when she realised exactly how thin the material was. She'd just have to brave the rain.

As soon as she stepped out onto the high street she heard Canner shout her name. Her first thought was that he'd come to drive her back to stop her from getting too wet. She had a joke about gentlemen not being extinct already on her lips, but she forgot it as soon as she saw the look on his face.

'Where have you been?'

The tone of his voice shocked her. 'Keeping out of the rain. Why?'

'I've been looking for you everywhere.'

'Obviously not,' she told him. 'Or you would have found me.'

He frowned at her. 'Come on, we've got to go.' He turned and walked quickly away, hunched up against the rain. He was impatient, agitated. 'I'm parked round the corner. I just hope I haven't been clamped.'

Amy had to hurry to keep up. 'What's wrong? Canner? Talk to me!' One thing she would never figure out was these mood swings. How many different people lived inside that head of his?

They turned the corner into the side street where they'd caught the runt who'd tried to steal her money, and she heard Canner swear. There was a traffic warden standing over a Sierra, writing out a ticket. Canner did a one-eighty on the spot and grabbed Amy's hand as he walked quickly back onto the high street, pulling her with him.

Amy was confused. 'What's wrong?'

But Canner wasn't paying her any attention; he was hovering, watching the traffic warden over her shoulder.

'Canner?'

'Tickets I can handle,' he said. 'But I don't know if traffic wardens can spot a nicked car or not with those little computer do-das of theirs. I really don't want to have to find something else in broad daylight if I can help it.'

Amy realised he must have got himself another car since they'd been to the restaurant. 'Didn't you fetch the car from the Italian?'

'Yeah, I did. But it—' He cut himself off, yanking on her arm. 'Come on.'

The warden had walked away. They hurried down the side street to the Sierra. Canner grabbed the ticket from under the windscreen wiper and ripped it up without even looking at it. 'Let's go.' He jumped into the driver's seat and scrabbled under the steering column for the wires.

'Are you going to tell me what's going on?' Amy stood her ground, refusing to follow orders from anybody until she knew why they were being given.

The car growled into life. Canner revved the engine loudly and shouted through the windscreen: 'I know who the thief is.'

She felt as though she'd been punched. The air went out of her. She rocked slightly on her heels to compensate. 'Who?'

'Come on!' Canner beckoned her into the car, annoyed by her slowness.

Now she obeyed, and Canner gunned the engine as the Sierra shot out into the rush-hour traffic of the high street.

They immediately got caught at a pedestrian crossing and he punched the steering wheel as two old ladies waddled their way across, barely able to contain the anger churning up his insides. He leaned forward over the wheel, squinting through smears left by the windscreen wipers. 'Come on. Come *on*!'

'Are you going to tell me who it is?' Amy asked. It was a whisper, as though it were a secret she was asking to be told.

'It's someone I've not trusted right from the very beginning.'

'You know him? You've met him?'

They leapt away from the lights while the green man was still flashing, drawing a few stares.

'Get this,' he said, his eyes flaring dangerously at her in the passenger seat. 'He's living in Crap Palace.'

The very idea rocked her again. 'What? Who?'

'That American: Riley.' He growled the name.

'He didn't sound American on the phone,' she said – then thought of the way he'd always mimicked her own accent when he spoke to her.

'Trust me. It's him.'

'How do you know?'

'Word got round he had some stuff to sell, one of the items being a top-of-the-range WAP phone. I stood outside his kip and called your mobile with mine, and heard yours ringing inside. Simple as that,' he snarled. 'Unbelievable.' He didn't stop for a junction and ignored the blaring of horns.

'Slow down!' Amy said. 'For God's sake, don't get me killed just as I'm about to get my things back.' She tried to take in what he'd told her. 'My things have been in the warehouse all this time? My rucksack and everything?'

'Unbelievable!' Canner repeated savagely. 'He arrived maybe an hour or two before you did last Tuesday night. He was probably already on his way here, nicked your stuff in Sheffield, and jumped on the first train.' He shook his head, cracking a tight smile. 'I've been phoning people in Leeds and Liverpool and bloody Glasgow, asking if anybody's seen your passport or a cash-card with the name Amy O'Connor. And all the time that American arsehole had it right under my nose.'

Amy stared at the wet road as it flashed by. She didn't know whether to feel angry or elated. To get her things back, after giving up hope – that was wonderful. But to think she'd spent a week with the thief within arm's reach. It made her shiver.

She looked at Canner gripping the wheel. She couldn't help being a little unnerved by his reaction. 'What are you going to do?'

'Get rid of him, that's what.' He was forced to stop at a set of traffic lights, but not without a squeal of complaint from the Sierra's brakes. 'And get back as much of your gear as I can.'

'How?'

He reached into his jacket's inside pocket and pulled out a clear plastic bag about the size of an envelope with half a dozen pills inside. He didn't look at her, kept his eyes on the road. She didn't want to touch them. She'd never seen drugs before, but knew instinctively that's what they were, though not what type exactly.

'Where did you . . .?'

'Same place I get a lot of stuff.' He put the small bag back inside his jacket. 'I can get anything, remember?' He slammed through the gears as he pulled away from the lights. 'Friends in low places, that's me. But not as low as Riley.' Saying the name twisted his mouth. 'I just have to plant them in his kip, fetch Lem, and he'll do the rest.'

'Can't you just explain about him stealing my rucksack?'

'*No drugs* is the only rule. Carrying is the only way to get kicked out. And anyway, who am I to try and kick someone out for stealing?' He almost grinned. Almost. 'This is the only way.'

She knew he usually parked on the other side of the docks, but today he drove as close to the warehouse as he could. He had to park on a patch of broken ground a few buildings over and around the rear. He couldn't get any closer because of the rubble strewn across the quayside road at the front.

'I think you should wait here,' he told her.

She didn't like that idea. 'Are you telling me what to do?'

'He'll recognise you. He's got your passport, hasn't he? So he's bound to know what you look like. I'd prefer it if he didn't know *why* he was being kicked out, as long as he gets the message he's not wanted.'

'What if he's seen me before?' This was the thought that unnerved Amy. He could have seen her every day for the last week, watched her, and she would never have known.

Canner was shaking his head. 'He would have said something, wouldn't he? You know, when you called him? Just to rub it in a bit, just to be extra smug. You've never hung around the centre with the others, and that's more or less the only time you get to meet anybody else. He hasn't got a clue what happened to you after he took your rucksack. And he doesn't give a damn. It'll be okay, yeah? You wait here.'

He slammed the car door and was gone.

Amy watched him disappear into a narrow alleyway between the empty buildings. She felt uncomfortable and useless. It seemed darker than it actually was because of the heavy rain clouds; the close spaces between the warehouses were becoming shadowy. She wasn't the sit-quietly-and-do-nothing type, never had been. She needed to feel some control. She watched the cloud limp across the sky, the spots of rain grow larger, thump louder on the windscreen. The boarded-up windows and padlocked doors of the derelict buildings looked as if their colours were being washed away.

She climbed out of her seat and paced around the car, ignoring the rain. The concrete was cracked and weeds grew green and brown against the grey. Broken glass, smashed wooden boards. She didn't dare hope too much about her rucksack – for all she knew the thief could have sold everything. He would certainly have spent the money in her wallet; cashed her travellers' cheques too.

She walked round and round the car, getting soaked.

The thought that a stranger had rummaged through her belongings – touching her clothes, looking at the picture in her passport, reading her name and address and date of birth, knowing so much about her – made her feel vulnerable and exposed. She suddenly thought somebody might be watching her now, from behind one of the broken shutters in a derelict warehouse, and climbed quickly back into the car.

She ran a hand through her wet hair, pulling strands of her fringe off her forehead. She realised she could walk past him in the street and she'd never know who he was. Yet *he'd* recognise *her*, and he'd know *everything* about her.

The thought made her shiver in her wet clothes. She sat with her knees hugged to her chest.

And suddenly she wanted to know something about *him* too. What type of person could make her feel the way he had? She remembered trying to make a picture of his face when she spoke to him on the phone. She needed to be able to see the person who had caused her so much pain, who had provoked so many tears.

So she followed the way Canner had gone.

She thought she'd hide and just watch. All she wanted to do was see for herself what he looked like. She'd watch him walk away and then she'd know what type of person he was. She'd see who'd managed to pull her world inside out. But as she emerged from one of the narrow cuttings onto the quayside road he was already there.

Canner, Kinard and the thief stood facing one another in

the falling rain. Three gunslingers. Canner saw her first. 'Amy . . .?' He stepped towards her.

But the thief, Riley, was quick enough to recognise her too. And he smiled as she approached. 'Amy?' he said, his voice sliding immediately into his spiteful imitation. 'Is that you? Darling, how wonderful to see you!'

She stared at him. He was nothing like she'd imagined. She felt an odd disappointment. He wasn't handsome, intelligent, charming. He was a disappointment.

'What a peculiar coincidence this is,' he was saying.

'You should check your gear,' Canner told her. 'We've made him leave everything in his kip.'

But all she could do was stare at the thief. He was an ugly, grotty little man.

And he seemed to understand now. A slow smile slid its way across his face. 'But there are no such things as coincidences, are there?' he said. 'Two add two. The missing piece of the jigsaw. You must be Mr Can Man's mystery woman, and making four, the one behind my eviction.' He bowed to her.

He was short, slump-shouldered, with a greasy ponytail and a pale, pock-marked face. He wore a baggy jumper, sagging with the rain, with a frayed hole in the left elbow. His long bony fingers had crescents of black dirt under the nails. And those fingers had crawled through her belongings like grubby spiders.

All she could do was stare at him. She was hollow inside, waiting to be filled up with some emotion or other. Maybe rage. She hoped it would be rage.

He returned her stare levelly.

Kinard looked awkward, unhappy. Canner tried to take Amy's arm but she shook him off.

'Why did you steal my rucksack?' she asked.

'Why are you such a sanctimonious bitch?' he asked.

'What?'

'Big word, eh? Who'da guessed I knew one.' His smile was pure slime. 'I was in Leeds,' he told her, facing her, ignoring Canner and Kinard. 'I heard about this warehouse where anybody was welcome, no questions asked. I hadn't eaten for two days – man, my stomach hurt so bad! I hopped on the first train I could, but got kicked off at Sheffield for not having a ticket. I cursed my bad luck, but it seemed as though fate was smiling on me after all. Because some sweet, pretty, but obviously stupid little girl went and left her fat rucksack full of goodies all alone on a bench. I was desperate for food and money. Did I tell you how bad my stomach hurt? And I didn't think twice because it was like a gift, just what I needed. Sweet, pretty, stupid little girl didn't look the starving type to me, and I reckoned she'd manage without.'

Canner moved threateningly towards Riley, but he didn't even blink. His eyes bored into Amy. She was rooted to the spot by what he was saying.

'And you have managed without, haven't you? Am I right, or am I right? Except you get your puppy-dog to do your stealing for you, don't you? Because you'd hate to break a nail doing any of the dirty work yourself.' He laughed at her. 'Why kick me out and sleep with him? Couldn't it just as easily be the other way around? I'm a real good hump – you better believe it!'

Now Canner made a grab at him, but the American easily side-stepped the move. He turned smoothly, quickly, like a boxer ready to fight. But Kinard was on his other side, and Riley stopped himself from throwing the punch his arm had been winding up to follow through. He held up his hands.

Amy watched it all in slow-motion. She was unable to move a muscle. Because everything he'd said . . . Hadn't it been the truth?

'I surrender,' Riley said to Kinard, stepping away, his arms still in the air. 'Hey, believe me. I've no quarrel with you, big guy. You're just the puppy-dog's plaything. Dumb but cute. And I bet you'd squeak too, if I bit you.'

He tried to wipe the rain from his face with the sleeve of his filthy jumper. He pulled back his sodden ponytail. He looked up to the sky as the rain poured down. Then he sneered at the three of them standing there. 'Ah, who gives a shit anyway?' he said. And walked away.

They watched him go; nobody said a word at first. Then Canner asked Kinard: 'Can you make sure he finds his way out of the docks, and manages to get far far away?'

Kinard nodded. 'But we're going to talk later about what happened here just now, aren't we?'

'Yeah,' Canner promised. 'We'll talk.' He took Amy's arm and led her back to the warehouse.

Amy was still waiting for the rage to fill her up; to drive her forward, to get her mouth working, get her shouting. But Riley's words were the only thing inside her at the moment. 'What he said was true, wasn't it?'

Canner ignored the question. 'Do you want to have a look for your things inside his kip?'

'Listen to me. He was right. We're all as bad as he is, aren't we? He stole my rucksack to be able to buy some food, and a ticket to get here.'

'That depends on whether or not you believe his story.'

'No it doesn't, not really,' she said. She shook her head because deep down believing his story had nothing to do with it. 'Even if he made the whole thing up, he's still not the only thief.'

'Let's just get your stuff,' Canner told her.

'I don't know if I want it any more, not after he's touched it. I know it sounds ridiculous . . .'

'Not to me.'

She sighed deeply. The hollowness inside her ached. 'I

want to go home,' she said. And as she admitted it a heavy weight seemed to lift from her shoulders. 'I want you to take the guitar back, and I want to go home.'

Canner didn't answer.

'I think I need to go home. I feel so tired. I've got to go soon. You know that, don't you?'

'Yeah,' he said quietly. 'I suppose I do.'

She dropped every last barrier she had, and threw away her shield. 'But you could come with me.' She felt him tense next to her and shrugged her shoulders. 'Why not?' She was looking at the dingy, rain-soaked buildings crowding around them. 'Got a better offer?'

He almost laughed. 'Not if you put it that way.'

'So?'

'So, I don't think I'd really fit in with your life back home, do you? What would your friends say if you turned up with me? What would your mum say?'

'You know something?' she said. 'I honestly don't care.' And she meant it too.

KING LEM

☉ne

'Who made *you* king of the castle?' the American sneered.

Lem stared hard at him, let his eyes burn into him. He wanted him to know he wasn't going to win this.

There was a crowd around them, everybody silent, watching. Lem turned to them and found Robbie's face. He glanced down at the kid's bandaged fingers, remembering the way they'd snapped like twigs under his brother's boot. Lem had been there. He'd seen it happen. He pointed at Robbie now. 'He made me king,' he said. He pointed at the Can Man. 'And so did he.' He pointed at other faces. 'And him. And her.' He included the whole crowd. 'All these people standing here, all these people under this roof. *They* made me king.'

The American continued to sneer. He wanted to break Lem in two; he wanted to pummel him into the floor. Lem could see it in his eyes, and by the considered way he moved, by the slow drags he took on his cigarette to mask how hot he was burning inside.

Lem stood his ground. And it *was* his ground. He wanted to say, 'I'm King of Crap Palace. And maybe I never asked for the role, and maybe it scares me sometimes, but for whatever reason I'm the one everybody trusts. So just back down now, because you can't win.'

He kept quiet because he knew the American wouldn't understand. Would probably never want to. And Lem wasn't about to waste his breath trying to explain it to him either. As far as he was concerned the American had broken the rule so he had to go. He was no longer welcome.

They stood there, trying to face each other down, trying to stare each other out. Mad dogs fighting for territory. But what the American didn't realise was that he wasn't the first. Lem had been here before, several times, and not once had he been forced to back down.

'I don't believe this, I'm not letting you kick me out onto the streets.'

Lem could tell the American was having trouble keeping himself in check. He wasn't stupid, far from it. He knew he was trapped: the only way to beat Lem was to knock him down in front of everybody; but everybody was on Lem's side. To conquer a king you have to defeat him in front of his subjects, yet his subjects will never love you for it.

He had to step down first. Had to. He had to let Lem win. As Lem had known he would all along.

'You're not welcome,' Lem told him. 'I don't want you here, they don't want you here. Get out!'

The American ground his teeth in frustration, ground his cigarette into the floor. 'You'll get yours,' he threatened quietly.

Canner and Kinard made sure he left, taking him downstairs and out into the docks. And the warehouse breathed again. Lem felt it.

He retreated upstairs.

He breathed again.

He slumped down into his armchair, its ancient musty smell always a comfort. But tonight the American had left a bad taste in his mouth. Lem's space was more or less the whole of the warehouse's top floor. It was enormous – wide, high, long, cavernous – but he squeezed himself into one corner. He felt safer being where the walls met.

There were two mattresses on the floor: he used one pushed up against one wall; if Canner slept up here he used the other. In between them was his armchair and a pile of half a dozen boxes crammed with books. He liked books, they got him through the rough patches. He used a small suitcase for his clothes. He had two gas heaters that he could aim where he wanted, and several of those roadwork lights. He had a desk with a small battery-operated tape-player on top surrounded by a scattering of tapes both in and out of their boxes. Next to the tapes was a stack of dog-eared notepads.

Because he was so high up, there were two shuttered windows he could open on warm days without being too worried about them being spotted. On the walls were the posters Canner had chosen; he seemed to think Lem needed them. There were a couple of arty-farty Dali ones, and one was of some band or other he'd never heard of but who Canner claimed were brilliant. The fourth was Buffy the Vampire Slayer. He kept them up to keep his friend happy.

It was not the kind of place that would turn up at the Ideal Homes exhibition – it was not quite *ideal* enough for most people. But then most people never even knew it existed, which was what made it ideal for Lem. He used it to get away from the world, and it had worked out okay for him so far.

He looked like a dosser, and doubted he smelled of roses any more. He was twenty, but most people would swear he was older. He certainly felt it. He used to be eighteen, living in a nice house, with a girlfriend and good enough grades to go to university. It had been a smooth, easy life. But he'd messed up somewhere down the line. And sometimes now he considered himself to be God's greatest living cliché: beware the walking stereotype. That was on bad days. Usually he just felt scared.

He reached for the book he was reading. It was his usual means of escape. The best way of forgetting nowadays, one of only two ways he had left to him. If the real world was getting a bit tough, he stepped out of it for a while. Time would hurry on, take him with it, but he'd never notice.

This book had been a present from Canner, and was his idea of a joke. *The Hunchback of Notre Dame*. This was the Can Man thinking he was real funny. But despite the hidden agenda Lem was enjoying it. It wasn't half bad for one of those old books.

Three chapters helped Time hurry along by maybe as much as an hour before he heard his friend. 'Enjoying it?'

He looked up to see Canner coming over from the stairs. 'Not half bad for one of those old books,' he admitted nonchalantly, not wanting to feed his friend's sarky humour any more than he had to. 'The American gone?'

Canner nodded quickly. 'A bit of a scene outside on the road,' he said. 'But Kinard's making sure he goes far far away.'

He dropped down onto his mattress with a grunt. The glow from the roadwork lights pushed awkward shadows across his face, but beneath them Lem could tell he was anxious. He didn't ask why. He knew Canner would only talk if he wanted to.

'What about you?' the Can Man asked. 'It was getting a bit tense down there at one point. How're you feeling?'

Lem sucked in a deep breath, inflated himself to fill the armchair. He let it out slowly and said: 'Self-righteous, superior, holier-than-thou.'

'All three?'

He nodded. He wanted to add 'hypocritical', but stayed quiet.

'Wow!' Canner rolled his eyes. 'Must be a good day.'

Lem put the book down and ran a hand through his hair. 'What're we doing here, Canner? What's going on?'

It was always the same question. Canner had more than likely been expecting it. So sticking to the script he shrugged and smiled and said: 'You're the boss. You tell me.'

But Lem knew he wasn't, not really. If he was the king then Canner was the parliament. Canner pulled the strings – he just didn't want anyone to know it. And now it looked as though he'd recruited Kinard as his general.

'You know, maybe we should stop letting people in,' Lem said. 'Maybe you should stop bringing them.'

'I can't do that,' Canner told him. 'And anyway, they're coming with or without me now. The word's spreading. Half the people down there have never even met me.'

'Doesn't it worry you?'

He shook his head. 'Should it?'

'It scares the hell out of me.'

Lem hadn't been the one to start bringing people here, he'd been too busy struggling with his own problems. He'd been far too full of self-pity to care about anyone else. Canner was the one turning up with kids, helping them build their kips and bringing them food. Lem had been too busy hiding in his corner. Canner was the one who'd transformed this derelict shell into a sanctuary. Lem had just played the part of the dumb hunchback campanologist.

The only thing that was Lem's was 'the rule', and that's why Canner had left it to him to enforce it.

'I need to talk to you about something,' Canner said. He forced himself to his feet by pushing on his knees with his hands. 'D'you want a drink?'

'Okay.'

'Okay, what? Okay the drink, or okay to talk?'

'Both.'

Canner nodded. 'Good.' He opened one of the desk's drawers and took out two mugs. He gestured at the notepads. 'How're your *memoirs*?'

Lem had to laugh. 'Please don't call them that,' he said. 'Call them trash, call them a waste of time, but for God's sake don't call them *memoirs*.' Writing was his other escape. Admittedly what he wrote more often than not made little sense to him, so what the rest of the world would make of those notepads he dreaded to think. But you had to have an ambition, right? You had to have some kind of dream to keep you going.

'You ever going to let me read any of it?' Canner asked.

'Doubt it.'

'I like a good romance myself.'

Lem nodded. 'And how *is* Amy, by the way?'

'She's what I want to talk about.' He was searching through other drawers. 'Where's that bottle I got you at the weekend?'

'It should be in there.'

'Yeah. Got it.' He retrieved a half-empty bottle of Pepsi from the bottom drawer. He ran his T-shirt around the stained rims of the mugs in a token attempt to wash them, then filled them both until the bottle was done.

Lem accepted his mug. The cola was warm and flat. Alcohol was not a means of escape. Not any more. He didn't dare. 'Are you staying with Amy again tonight?' he asked. 'Poor Shelly's going to start thinking she's doubly homeless.'

Canner grinned at him. 'You've got a spare mattress up here,' he said with a wink.

'She's not really my type,' Lem said quickly, making his friend laugh out loud.

'She's okay once you get to know her.'

'I'll have to take your word on that one. Personally, she reminds me a bit too much of a praying mantis.'

Canner laughed again. 'Okay, I'll give you that.' But then he sighed. 'No, I'm not staying with Amy. Not tonight. I think she needs a bit of time by herself.'

'Everything okay?'

He looked uncomfortable again, but Lem couldn't figure out what it was.

'A couple of people have searched Riley's kip. It looks like he's the reason Amy's in here, because he's the one who nicked all her stuff in the first place. And not just hers. I think some of the stuff other people have lost recently has ended up in that kip too.'

'That's why you wouldn't let him take anything with him,' Lem said. Canner nodded, and Lem began to think he could see where this conversation was headed. He asked: 'So has Amy got everything back?'

'Not really. You know – obvious stuff, like cash and travellers' cheques and that, she's not got a hope of getting back, so she's still broke. But just things like getting her phone and her passport seem to have sorted her out a bit.'

'So she's leaving?'

Canner nodded slowly, sipping his flat cola.

Lem knew him well enough to realise how much he liked this girl. Despite all the books he'd read he'd never really believed in love at first sight: it was simply a poor writer's tool to advance the plot, wasn't it? But he reckoned Cupid had certainly put one over on the Can Man recently. He knew his friend was going to miss her. He also knew he'd never got himself so personally involved with anyone in the warehouse before. Yes; he brought many of them here. And yes, he helped them out where he could by getting them what they needed. But usually Crap Palace itself did the healing by giving them the space. This time, however, Canner had met someone different, someone special. It was going to hurt him just about as bad as it could to see her go.

But Lem owed Canner – well, probably owed him dozens. He'd be there for his best friend when she left. He'd make sure of that.

'When's she leaving?'

Canner finished his Pepsi in one last gulp. 'Not till next week. She's still got to get a bit of money together, so she reckons middle of next week at the earliest before she's got enough.'

'Come up here when she's gone,' Lem told him. 'We'll put some depressing music on, get a little morbid and stuff. Bitch at the world like we used to do in the old days, and shout about how crap life is. It always made us feel better back then.'

But Canner was shaking his head. 'I really like her, Lem. I've never met anyone like her before, no matter how crappy that sounds.' He looked up, and only now could Lem read the look on his face. All of a sudden he could tell what was coming next.

'I'm going with her,' Canner said.

The news hit the king hard.

Two ☉

Suddenly his eyes were open. He'd been fast asleep, dead to the world, dreaming maybe, but his eyes had popped open and now he was wide awake. The darkness of his space in the warehouse felt different somehow. He rolled onto his back and held his watch close to his face, pressing for its little light with the other hand.

00:00.

If it was bomb it was about to go *boom*! This was Ground Zero. Goodbye to all that. If it was really his watch, however, this was the start of the first day of the rest of his life. He held his breath. Which one? Which one?

00:01 and no big bang.

He let his arms flop down by his side, trying not to feel too disappointed. But there was something not quite right. He didn't know what had woken him. Even in the pitch darkness he knew his space so well that he could tell something was different about it tonight. He lay very still, but strained his eyes and ears. At the sound of the footstep he jumped up off the mattress and grabbed the torch from by his pillow.

Its beam leapt forward, a fuzzy cone of light spilling across the wooden floorboards. Someone was running at him, pounding footsteps in the dark. He swung the torch like a sabre, slashing at the blackness. He caught the edge of someone's bulk charging towards him.

'Kinard?'

But when he swung the beam back he didn't recognise the

face. He had time to take in the short, spiky dreadlocks as he was slammed to his knees, his breath exploding out of him. He couldn't keep hold of the torch. It skittered across the floorboards, its beam spinning like a manic lighthouse. He saw the huge shadow over him, was kicked in the chest, knocked flat. Then the shadow was raising a thick arm and heavy fist. There was something in that fist. At the last second he tried to turn his face away but still caught a glancing blow. The skin of his cheek tore open; the bone rang with pain like a bell.

He howled and kicked out savagely, not knowing where his bare feet were landing, but feeling the shadow stumble away with a grunt.

He was able to stand. He fumbled for the roadwork lights. He managed to get two on before his attacker was on him again. Lem could see him more clearly now, could see he was wearing a combat-green muscle T-shirt and an elaborate dragon tattoo at the top of one arm. He saw that he had a bike chain wrapped around his fist.

Again Lem was charged to the floor, but he was quick to roll away. He grabbed for the nearest light and swung it hard, shattering its plastic casing against his attacker's shins, making him cry out, step away. Lem struggled up again. He wanted his jeans. He wanted his knife.

Dragon Man unwrapped the chain from his fist and started swinging it around his head like a flail. Lem threw the whole light at him, grabbed a second one that was close by and hurled that too. He snatched up a handful of books, threw them. He made as if to run for the stairs, waited for Dragon Man to commit himself to cutting him off, then dodged back to his armchair and snatched up his jeans. His knife was in the back pocket.

'Come on, then. *Come on!*' He moved into the weak orange light and made sure Dragon Man could see the open blade. 'You want some, you big bastard? So come and get some. *Come ON*!'

His attacker was just a silhouette now: Lem couldn't see his eyes, but could sense his hesitation.

Lem was shaking, adrenaline and pain making him shiver with tense heat. 'COME ON! COME ON THEN!' He was nowhere near as big as Dragon Man, so he aimed to make himself twice as loud, twice as aggressive. It was his only means of defence.

Dragon Man wrapped the bike chain around his fist again. Keeping his face towards Lem at all times he moved over to the desk and smashed his fist into the tape-player, smashed the lights that were close by, kicked over one of the heaters. He had a cigarette-lighter. When he flicked it alight Lem could see his face above the flame. The eyes were scarily passive. He dropped the lighter onto Canner's mattress and the sheets immediately caught. He then turned his back and walked away, swinging the chain by his side, almost in time with his strides.

Lem couldn't move. He was shaking so badly he felt he might not be able to balance if he tried to walk. He watched Dragon Man's shadow all the way to the stairs. He could feel blood from his cheek running down his neck, soaking into his already grubby T-shirt. He thought he might cry. The wave of delayed fear was so great he almost wept.

But the flames on Canner's mattress were growing; the light they threw reached out across the whole of Lem's space, as if checking out the best way to spread. He hated fire. Fire had always scared him. He loathed bonfire night. One November the Fifth when he was a kid he'd seen a house where they'd been throwing a firework party in the back garden burn to the ground, and set light to its next-door neighbour on the way. Fire was too wild, too unpredictable. He preferred radiators.

He dropped his knife and on legs like soft springs managed to grab the end of the mattress and pull it out from the corner towards the centre of the floor, away from the walls and books and desk. Then he went looking for help.

Kinard was coming up the stairs as he was heading down. 'I think I just saw Riley's mate . . .' Either the look on Lem's face or the bloodied state of it plugged the rest of the words solidly in his mouth. He just stared.

'There's a fire. I need your help.'

Maybe Kinard's words had failed, but his mind was in perfect working order. He ran past Lem up the stairs and straight over to the burning mattress. He took hold of one side and flipped it over, smothering the flames. He stamped on a few more resilient orange and red fingers clawing their way around the edges. Lem joined him, stamping on the glowing embers.

Kinard stared hard at him when they were done. 'You okay?'

Lem couldn't lie, so asked instead: 'Who did you say he was?'

'Guy called Jan, the American's bosom buddy. I'm sorry, Lem, I didn't see him going up. I only saw him come down. I would've . . .'

'Not your fault.'

Kinard hung his head, stamped on already dead ashes. 'I'll make sure he's gone for good.'

'I'd appreciate that.' Lem had meant it to sound light, but he was in no mood to try too hard.

'Do you want me to pay him back for you?'

Lem considered it. But wouldn't that be the beginning of a tight spiral of revenge? Dragon Man was here for revenge for the American, Kinard would get revenge for him, then someone else might go for Kinard. 'No. Leave it,' he said. He touched his cheek. The blood on his fingers looked strange in the orange glow from the roadwork lights. Not like blood at all.

'You should see Stef,' Kinard told him. 'She might have something to patch you up.'

'I should see a doctor,' Lem replied. Then: 'I'll be okay.'

Kinard was still hanging his head. He looked uncomfortable, but Lem had too many other things to worry about right now to think about Kinard. His head was spinning too much with his own thoughts and worries. 'I should get some sleep,' he said, heading for his corner.

Kinard followed a little way. 'I need to talk to you. It's about what happened last night . . .'

Last time someone had said they needed to talk it had been Canner telling him he was leaving. He didn't want to hear any more of that kind of talk. 'Can you save it, Kinard? Later, okay?'

Kinard shrugged. Reluctantly he turned to go.

'Don't say a word about this to anyone. Canner'll find out, because he comes up here. But no-one else. I don't want Get Well cards.'

Kinard nodded slowly, and left him alone.

Lem sat in his armchair, staring at the floor. He was still shaking, a trembling in his hands he couldn't quite calm no matter how hard he clasped them together.

THREE

Lem felt no real passage of time in the warehouse. He believed you only noticed the days, the weeks, the months passing by if you took a moment to yourself to stand still and look around.

He thought of Time as a river that carries you along, its current forever hurrying you forward. You never notice how quickly the flow is rushing you onward unless every now and again you plant your feet firmly in the sandy river bed and feel the waters surging around you. It is in these moments that you can take a look at where you've been, and even try to see where you might be going. But the current is very strong, and you can only ever resist it for a moment before it picks you up off your feet again and hurries you ever on.

Lem never took that moment to plant his feet, to feel Time splash around him push against him. He didn't fight against the current. He lay on his back, his arms spread wide, staring up at the sky, and let it bear him ever forward.

Maybe that's why Canner's decision to leave frightened him so much. Because it was going to force him to take that moment to look around – to see where he'd been, to look where he might be going.

'You can't keep doing this to me, Canner. This isn't fair.'

'On who? On Lucy?'

Lem pushed past him and headed upstairs to his space.

Canner followed close behind. 'What do you want me to do? Kick her out when she's just got here? I'll go kick her out, shall I?'

Lem span round at the top of the stairs, eyes suddenly blazing, and jabbed a finger in the Can Man's chest. 'Don't get like this with me, Canner. I'm warning you. Don't you dare!' He strode across the floor towards his corner.

Canner still followed, skirting round the edge of his burned mattress. 'Lucy's in now,' he said. 'Robbie's let her have the bigger kip. I can't say, "Sorry, Lucy, but Lem's feeling a bit hard done by at the minute. Can you come back later? I'm sure the doorway you've been sleeping in for the past two nights is safe enough, really. Don't worry about those big men who've been—"'

'Stop it, Canner, okay? Just shut up!' The fight had deserted Lem as quickly as it had appeared. His armchair welcomed him with a sigh of its old cushions. He touched his cheek, scratched at the plasters covering the wound. Fortunately it looked worse than it actually was, but it hurt plenty. He took his hand from his cheek and put it into his jeans pocket, where it had been most of the day, curled around the knife.

'I don't see what the problem is all of a sudden.' The Can Man stood facing him. 'Are you really wanting to turn her away?'

'Of course not.'

'Well, then. Where's the problem?'

'Things have changed.'

'Because of what happened to your face last night? Or because I'm leaving?'

'Either of those is as good a place to start as any, I suppose. Yes, because you're leaving. But yes, because of what happened last night. Choose either. Things are getting out of hand, Canner. Have you seen how many there are down there? New people are coming every day. It's like there's some massive queue somewhere. Lucy – she's not the problem. She's just another one. And tomorrow there'll be one more.'

'People need somewhere to go,' Canner said.

'That's exactly what I'm trying to say.'

'I don't—'

Lem wouldn't let him speak. 'It was Robbie,' he said. 'The other night. He sat there letting Stef bandage the fingers his brother had just crippled, and he refused to go to the police. He just didn't see it as an option, it hadn't even crossed his mind. His father is who knows where, his mother next to worthless, his teachers probably don't even know his name. Talk about slipping through the net!'

'So it was lucky he had this place.'

'Look, Canner. I owe you a lot, okay? So much even God's going to have a tough time accounting for it all when I die. I love you like a brother, and all that stuff. But what you've started here scares me half to death.'

'You're worried because of last night. Bloody hell, Lem, I'd've been bricking it too.'

'I didn't even know his name, I'd never even met him before. I know less than half the people down there nowadays. But that's not the point. I don't need protection. I can handle myself fine. What scares me most is you leaving. This time next week you'll be up in Durham or wherever the hell Amy's from. But me, I'm the one left here.'

'There's Kinard. Stef. Maybe even Robbie now.'

'But everybody looks up to *me*. Everybody thinks *I'm* in charge.'

Canner nodded. 'Yes they do.'

'So, don't you get it? Have you forgotten the state I was in this time last year?'

'No,' Canner said simply. Then: 'I haven't forgotten about the state Robbie was in either. Or Shelly, Brodie, Tilman. Even Kinard. I can't sleep at night for thinking about the first time I saw Kinard. Jesus, that scared *me*.' Canner was pale with the memory. 'But where else was he going to go if I hadn't brought him here. Like the rest of them, if parents or teachers or social workers or whoever had given half a shit, I'm sure they'd have gone to them first. As it was, I could bring them here.'

'But that's the point, isn't it? *You're* going.'

'I've told you before, word's spreading, people are finding this place by themselves.'

'And every one of them is going to be looking up to me.'

'You're the boss,' Canner told him.

'No I'm not. That's what I'm trying to say. It's been you, Canner. All along, it's been you.'

'You're the king.'

'You forced me to be.'

'It's your rule.'

Lem let a gasp of breath go from his lungs. 'And you know why it's my rule, don't you?'

Canner nodded slowly. 'Because you came here to get yourself clean.' The look on his face acknowledged the care needed if they were going to talk about it.

'And you know why I had to get myself clean?'

Canner didn't speak.

Lem looked him deep in the eyes. For all of the time they'd spent together, this was the one thing Lem had never opened up about – maybe because it would mean having to look back to see where he'd been. It wasn't a particularly original story; he was certain it had been told before, just with different names. He was a walking stereotype, don't forget. But . . .

He'd been perfect once, or at least thought he was. He'd breezed through exams, he always had one girl or another on the go who'd put out for him, and he was in the school football and basketball teams. He'd had so many friends he couldn't remember all their names. Teachers loved him. His parents were so proud. Mr Popular, that was him. Easy life, that was him. The perfect boy. But he'd been bored out of his brain.

So: drugs.

Because he was 'bored'. Kind of pitiful, really.

He could almost feel the rushing river of Time tugging at his legs, wanting to carry him on, wanting him to forget again. But he kept his feet. He held his ground and looked back. 'It was because of Joe,' he said. 'I got myself clean because of my best friend Joe.'

He waited for some kind of reaction from Canner, although he wasn't sure what. Maybe laughter, maybe disdain. Maybe the Can Man would simply up and leave right this very minute because he couldn't give a monkey's toss for past lives. But no, Canner didn't even bat an eye.

Lem shrugged, continued. 'I had the inevitable "fall from grace". You've heard it so many times before from other people, I'm sure. Stealing from parents, tears before bedtime, waking up on the stinking, filthy floor of a public toilet. And I didn't have the strength or the inclination to do anything about it because I could never see the state I was in. Far too mashed for that. I was like a vampire, casting no reflection. And feeding off others. Feeding off people like Joe, who I'd always claimed was my best friend.'

His voice cracked. He snapped his teeth shut to hold the sound in. Canner still hadn't moved, but he was taking in every word. There was a glistening in his eyes which Lem had to turn away from or he wouldn't have been able to continue.

'About the only thing I did see at the time was what happened to Joe. I got him involved. I introduced my oldest friend to the fun world I was living in by giving him half a pill for his birthday. I got him high, got him right up there with the birds. And he was a natural. He was never coming down.

'I heard this statistic once, that it takes three days for your system to clear acid – you know, three days for a tab to wear off fully. But you can still have flashbacks for the rest of your life, apparently. Don't know how true it is, it's just something I heard. Maybe I read it in one of my books.' He waved at the box with a loose hand, not that Canner followed the gesture. 'But me and Joe loved to drop a bit of acid, no matter what other insane cocktail of junk was already inside us. You name it, we did it, anything and everything. Didn't give two damns for statistics back then.

'We went to this open-air gig near Sheffield. Don't ask me who was playing, because I haven't got a clue. Very probably didn't have at the time either. On top of whatever else he was doing at the time, I saw Joe swallow four tabs in three hours. Number five was a disappointment – it wasn't getting to him quick enough any more.'

Lem shook his head, tried to hold onto his voice. 'So he lay back, lay out on the grass in the sun, and put numbers six and seven on his eyeballs. Do you know what that's like? Seeing someone you love do that to themselves? And feeling like it was your fault anyway? It scared me so bad. He just lay there, his eyes rolled up into the back of his head so all I could see was the whites. He was really quiet. But I didn't dare think about what was going on inside his head – his mind could have been tearing itself apart for all I knew. And I was watching it happen.' He took a shaky breath.

'Seeing him just – I don't know . . . I couldn't take it. Look what I'd done to my best friend! I just couldn't bear seeing what was happening to him. I still don't know where he is, how he is. I just walked out on him. I don't know whether he's still alive or not. I messed up my best friend's life, and walked away.'

He still wouldn't look at Canner. And Canner still hadn't moved or tried to speak. Lem stared hard at the floor.

He'd come to the warehouse sometime in early September. 'Cold turkey'. Canner found him here. Lem could hear him most nights racing the stolen cars along the quayside, up and down for hours at a time. He didn't have a clue when Canner first started bringing others here. He'd already got Lem the mattress and the chair by then. Some books too. But he just woke up one day to hear hammering coming from downstairs, and when he went to find out what was happening he saw a kid nailing doors together to build a kip.

The lad had actually shaken his hand, and said: 'You're Lem, right? Thanks for letting us stay.' As if Lem owned the place. He had a girl with him. And Lem kicked her out three weeks later for shooting up. He told Canner he could bring who he wanted to, just no drugs.

'I think it's the rule that matters,' Canner told him. 'People come here because of your rule. They see a place free of drugs as a safe place.'

Lem touched his cheek. It was just as effective, but less hard work than thinking of a sarcastic comeback. 'But that's not the reason I said no drugs in the first place. I don't hate drugs, I'm probably their biggest fan. I wanted to take everything that girl had on her and run away. I said no drugs because I don't trust myself around them. I don't even drink any more because I just daren't take the risk of getting drunk and then wanting to go out to get high.'

'You're clean now. It's all behind you.'

'Come on, Canner. Spare me the platitudes. I'm twenty years old, okay? And I've only just managed to admit responsibility for my own life, so how can I handle other people's.'

'You don't have to. They come here to get the space to do it for themselves.'

'What am I going to tell Robbie if his brother catches him down the street one night?' Lem asked.

'People need someone to look up to. Everyone needs some kind of king or boss or big brother. It's a good feeling when you know someone's looking out for you. Isn't it kind of what you've been doing anyway? Everybody follows you.'

'Only because you pushed me out front.'

'What happened last night . . . it wasn't your fault. There's more to it . . .'

Lem was shaking his head. 'Look, I'm sorry, Canner. I'm not you. And I don't think I can do it without you. I don't want to be responsible. When you go, I go. I'm closing the warehouse down. Or at least my part in it anyway.' The Can Man opened his mouth to speak but Lem wouldn't let him. 'I'm not a king or a boss or a big brother,' he said. 'I'm just a fuck-up too.'

FOUR

Lem had written a short story called 'Perfect Sam' about a man who was undoubtedly the most perfect person in the whole world. But nobody around him, neither his friends nor his family, nor even Sam himself, realised it.

In the story a lot of people talked about perfection. They agreed that some handsome hunk with a beautifully sculptured face and chiselled jaw and big muscles, who was super-intelligent and talented at every sport and every creative art, was very probably the perfect example of a human being. On the flip-side, someone who was blind, or missing a kidney or something, or wheelchair-bound, dependent on carers; or someone who simply suffered with an allergy; someone who was not too bright, or wore glasses, or stuttered, or was simply seriously ugly, would be deemed impaired.

The people in the story had only one version of perfection, but dozens and dozens of imperfection. And yet they were wrong.

Nobody took any notice of Sam because he was neither of the extremes: he was average. Nobody realised that he was perfect. He was exactly as God/nature had intended. He wasn't gorgeous or hideous looking, he was okay. He had a girlfriend who would become his wife and mother of his children. His heart was healthy and ticked at exactly the right speed to see him through a long life. He was clever enough to earn money to buy food to stay alive and afford a warm place to live. He wasn't muscle-bound, but neither was he weak; he was simply as strong as he needed to be. He wasn't tall or short, fat or thin. He was exactly what a human being had evolved to be and needed to be, and was therefore perfect.

But that made him fairly dull and easily forgettable to most people (which was fine because he only needed love from his friends and family anyway – no more, no less). And at the end of the story Sam died quietly, painlessly, happily at the age of seventy-four.

Lem had once thought he was perfect, when he was the centre of attention at school. Nowadays he was finding it difficult just to be average.

He was re-reading this old story of his when Kinard appeared. 'We need you downstairs. We've got a problem.'

Lem quickly buried the notebook he was reading in the middle of the pile. His first reaction was: 'Where's the Can Man?' Too late he tried to bite the words back.

Kinard shook his head. 'Out somewhere. I haven't seen him since—'

'No, it's okay. I'm coming.' His reliance on Canner was sometimes so strong it was crippling. He forced himself towards the stairs. 'Is someone carrying?'

Again Kinard shook his head. 'A bit more complicated.'

Downstairs there was a small group gathered around the centre. They reminded Lem of gawpers at a road accident. He cursed Canner for not being around. This was exactly the kind of grief Lem didn't want, couldn't handle, but he took a deep breath and waded into the middle. What he saw shocked him in a way he wasn't expecting.

There was a little kid sitting on the floor, staring up at the tall strangers around him. He didn't appear to be particularly nervous, just bewildered. He was wearing immaculate blue dungarees, with a crisp white T-shirt underneath, and a base-ball cap. His bright, freshly washed clothes were as jarringly out of place as his age. He saw Lem, saw the badly covered wound on his cheek and shied away.

But Lem was backing away too. He turned to Kinard. 'What's going on?'

'He just wandered up the stairs,' Kinard said. 'Someone found him roaming around the kips. He says his name's Michael.'

Lem felt his world tip on its axis slightly. He could have been watching himself on TV. He stared at the little kid, and the kid stared back. 'Can't you get rid of him?'

'He said he's looking for someone called Lem.'

'What?' The world just about tipped all the way over, and Lem barely managed to keep his balance. 'I've never seen him before in my life. I wouldn't even—'

'Are you Lem?' the little boy asked. His voice was strong, quite bold for someone so young and out of place.

Lem could feel the gathered group of people watching him; watching their king. He looked hard at the boy, searching his memory against the boy's face, racking his brain for younger brothers of old friends. But that in itself was ridiculous because it still didn't tell him how on earth the kid had managed to get here anyway. He turned to look at the others around him, not that any of them could help either.

He held up his hands in a small gesture of surrender – not to the kid, but to the situation. Just roll with it, he told himself, because there was nothing else he could do.

'Yeah, I'm Lem.' He crouched down to the boy's level. 'And you're Michael, right?' The boy nodded. 'Do you know me, Michael?'

Michael seemed to think about it for a long time before shaking his head.

'But you know my name, don't you? How come?'

'He told it to me.'

'Who?' Lem was looking around, but Michael wasn't pointing.

'The man who said I could come here.'

Lem leaned in a little closer. 'Do you know who the man was? Do you know his name?' Michael shook his head and Lem tried a different tack. 'Why did he say you could come here?'

'Because I wanted a PlayStation, but Daddy got me a bike. I didn't want a bike.' He shook his head again to prove it.

Lem nodded, even though it didn't mean a thing to him. 'Bike's are all right,' he tried. Jesus Christ! What was he talking about? What the hell was . . .? He decided to start again. 'How old are you, Michael?'

'I'm six.'

'Hey! That's great. Can you guess how old I am?'

Michael clearly didn't give a damn. 'It's my birthday today. And I'm six.' He was proud to be so old.

Lem felt as though he were well and truly drowning here. Again he looked for help from the others; again to no avail. 'Happy birthday,' he mumbled. And it set off a quiet echo among everybody gathered, which in itself was surreal enough to make him want to laugh. He managed to bite his tongue.

'I wanted a PlayStation but Daddy bought me a bike, so I ran away.'

'You ran all the way here?' Lem asked.

Michael shook his head hard enough to tilt his cap at an odd angle. 'No!' He was obviously upset that Lem had forgotten already. 'The 'merican man said all people that run away come here.'

Lem tensed. Kinard was at his shoulder.

'And Lem looks after them. The 'merican said Lem would get me a PlayStation.'

'The man was American? An American brought you here?'

Either the sudden tenseness in his voice, or maybe seeing Kinard lurch at him, made Michael's face crease in fear. Lem couldn't help it – he reached out instinctively to stop the boy in case he was going to run, and grabbed hold of him by the front of his dungarees. 'The American, Michael. Tell me about the American.'

The little boy's eyes slowly widened, his bottom lip trembled.

'What about the *American*?'

And with something of a delayed reaction the boy burst into tears.

Lem let him go as if he was on fire and backed off quickly, standing up. He swore at himself for being so clumsy.

'I want to go home,' Michael sobbed.

'Okay, Michael, don't worry. We'll take you home,' Lem assured him, dropping his voice again, softening it. He looked around. 'Can somebody take him home?' he said. 'Or even drop him at McDonald's or something. Somewhere safe. If his parents or the police are given directions here and find him, we're really screwed.'

A girl volunteered – someone else Lem didn't recognise, but he didn't stop her. She crouched down next to the little boy to coax him out of his tears.

'Just leave her to it,' Lem told everyone else. 'Give her some space, the kid's frightened enough.' Thanks to me, he thought. He ducked his head and turned to leave, but Kinard had a hand on his arm.

'I really need to have that talk with you, Lem.'

He sighed. 'Upstairs then,' he said, and led the way.

He was peculiarly shaky on his feet. He hadn't enjoyed that experience. Hadn't enjoyed it at all. The American was bearing his grudge big time. Dumping missing six-year-olds in Crap Palace was one step too close to crazy for Lem's liking. It felt as if there was a bomb ticking, and soon it was bound to go off. No way Lem would be able to stop it.

He flopped down into his armchair. Kinard hovered.

'I don't know if I can help . . .' Lem started.

'It's about Riley,' Kinard said. 'The American, yeah?'

'Do you know where he is?'

Kinard shook his head. He looked anxious, pained by what he had to say. 'Look, Lem, I don't want to be a grass or anything, but Canner lied to you. He set Riley up. He planted those pills on him just so you'd kick him out. He wasn't carrying at all.'

Lem's world lurched from one swing of its axis to another. His hand went straight to the wound on his cheek. He could have been punched – the shock hurt just as bad. He tried not to let it show too much, but Kinard was no fool. 'I'm not going to call you a liar, Kinard. But, you know, you are sure about this, aren't you?'

Kinard nodded in that slow, ponderous way of his. 'Canner knew Riley had Amy's stuff, so set him up for you to kick him out. He . . .'

And with the worst (or maybe the best) timing possible, Canner chose that exact moment to appear at the top of the stairs. 'Hey, Lem. I just heard you made a new buddy.'

Kinard stepped quickly aside, eyes cast down.

Lem watched his friend walk towards him, and there was a real knot of hurt tightening in his stomach. No anger, not yet. He just felt cheated. It was more painful than anger because it was more difficult to release. It was a hollow, empty feeling. He stood up slowly.

Canner noticed the look on his face. 'You okay?'

'I told him about Riley,' Kinard said.

Canner slowed his stride across the floor. He took a deep breath. 'Right.' He nodded to himself. 'Okay. I guess I've got some explaining to do, then.'

'Don't bother,' Lem told him.

'Come on, hear me out at least.'

'Honestly, Canner. There's no need. It's all turned to crap now anyway.'

Kinard was watching the two of them closely.

'You what? What has? Don't talk rubbish. I wanted him out – he was a trouble-maker. A Yankee prick. It wasn't just Amy's gear in his kip, you know.'

'Why didn't you tell me?'

'Because you wouldn't have kicked him out if he wasn't carrying.'

'Probably not, no.'

Canner was by his side now. 'Look, I'm sorry, Lem. I wasn't happy about doing it. And I know a lot of people will call me a hypocrite for wanting to get rid of a thief, but he was stealing from people in here. From *us*. From the people who have sod all as it is, because that's why they're in here.'

What Canner was saying made some sense to Lem. But there was a kind of betrayal here as well, wasn't there? 'I thought we were meant to be able to trust each other.'

Canner was stung. 'I've never let you down. You can't name me one time I've ever let you down.'

Lem touched the wound on his cheek again. 'What about this?' he asked. 'I took this because of you. Because the American must think I knew what was going on all along.' He could feel the anger now, building inside him. 'Some bloke I'd never even set eyes on before was sent to do me some serious damage because of your lies, and you reckon you've never let me down? Jesus!'

'Look, Lem . . .' Canner tried, reaching out to take his shoulder.

But Lem shrugged him off nastily. 'Don't, Canner. Just get out, okay? I'm not—'

'Lem, I . . .'

'Leave it, Canner. Don't . . .'

But Canner tried to take his shoulder again, and something inside Lem snapped. He swung for his best friend, his full weight behind the punch, snarling like an angry dog. He would have connected too, if Kinard hadn't stepped in the way and caught his forearm across his massive chest. The punch fell limp.

Canner looked shocked by Lem's action. It was the last thing in the world he'd expected. He took a step back. And Lem felt guilty, but was still too angry to admit to it.

Kinard moved to the side again and Lem sat back down. 'So why couldn't you trust me with this?' he asked.

Canner took time to collect himself. 'I did it for Amy,' he said. 'And maybe it wasn't the best move I've ever made. But . . . But I don't know . . .' He threw up his hands. 'But I wish I did. Look, you're big enough and ugly enough to sort yourself out now, no matter what you say. Amy was in that position where she needed someone there.'

Lem couldn't help feeling jealous of Amy. She had his last good friend.

Nobody looked at each other. Nobody knew how to ease the tension.

Eventually Kinard spoke up. 'It's this place I'm worried about. Riley's got it in for us. For whatever reason, that doesn't matter. But what with his mate having a go at you, Lem, and now this little kid being dumped here, he just wants to ruin everything for us. What if he tells someone about us? What's stopping him from going to the police? He knows everything about us – how we stay hidden, how we handle patrols; everything.'

The three of them were quiet, each letting Kinard's words sink in. They went pretty deep into Lem. All the way down. He might have decided he was leaving, but he had been assuming that Crap Palace would carry on. It was so important to him that the warehouse survived. His time here was all he had left – the only thing that mattered any more. Crap Palace had to go on doing what it did for people whether he was here or not.

When he looked up at Canner, it was obvious his friend was thinking the exact same thing. The warehouse was what mattered most. They'd both do whatever they could to ensure it survived.

'What're we going to do?' Kinard asked.

Lem said: 'This American . . . Riley – whatever his name is – we need to get to him before he can do any serious damage. He must still be around, somewhere in town still. We have to get to him as quick as possible.' He sat in his armchair as though it was a throne and took the decision. He turned to Canner. 'Can you find him?'

The Can Man nodded.

FIVE

On that same Saturday afternoon little Michael was taken to McDonald's and left with the staff, with the explanation that he'd been found wandering in the car park. Lem waited. He waited for the American's next stunt, he waited for Michael's parents to bring the police down on the warehouse. He knew it was what the American wanted. They were meant to be scared. He was toying with them. The police were the biggest fear: Lem knew they'd have a field day in this place. A dozen missing person files would be solved with a single glance around the kips, a dozen shoplifting cases solved in a second. It would be a copper's Christmas and birthday presents rolled into one.

Of course, all this would be easy to blame on Canner. But Lem couldn't bring himself to believe it was his friend's fault. He was the last person to want to jeopardise Crap Palace. He'd built this place in the very beginning. He knew Canner was suffering because of the mistake he'd made. He'd been out all day yesterday and the day before, long into the night, his ear to the ground, his eyes open, trying to find the American. Lem had wondered whether it was simply to keep out of his way, but deep down he knew that Canner refused to see what he'd created be destroyed. The Can Man was trying to make things right again. Lem only hoped the two of them could stop it all from crumbling down around them.

But the day of Amy's departure drew closer. Would Canner go with her if the warehouse wasn't safe? Would Lem stay on without him to ensure its safety? Neither answer was within reach for the king.

On the Tuesday the American was found.

This was the Can Man's third car in a fortnight: an old-style Astra. Lem had asked Canner not to approach the American by himself; to come and get him first. Now he was sitting in the passenger seat, gripping the upholstery, as they headed out of the docks and onto the dual carriageway – not because Canner was a bad driver, but because this was the first time he'd set foot outside the warehouse in daylight for a long, long time. He felt like a vampire.

'How'd you find him?' he asked.

'I talked to Smelly George,' Canner replied. 'You know, the leaflet guy. He knows most of the waifs and strays around here. Apparently Riley's holed up in a squat with a couple of the lads he has working for him.'

'Where?'

'Straw Street. I left Kinard wandering around, to keep an eye on things. He'll call us if he spots Riley or his big mate.'

By daylight the town seemed bigger than Lem remembered. He stayed slumped in his seat, worried someone he knew would see him. Or he'd see them. So he kept his eyes on the dashboard. 'How're we going to play this?' he asked.

Canner seemed surprised. 'I thought you had it all worked out.'

'Not a clue,' Lem admitted. 'I just know we've got to get him to keep his mouth shut.'

'That's not going to be easy.'

Lem shook his head. No it wasn't. Maybe talking wasn't going to be enough. He had his knife in his back pocket.

Canner parked in the next street over. Kinard was waiting for them on the corner of Straw Street. It was a hot day, big round sun. Lem was glad Kinard was here: he could always hide in the big guy's shadow if all hell broke loose.

'Seen anybody?' Canner asked. They looked along the street, cars parked up on the pavement bonnet to boot, ill-kept terraced houses on either side. Several FOR SALE signs marking rotten bay windows.

Kinard shook his head. 'Nobody's been in or out. You're sure this is the right place, yeah?' The squat was just over halfway down, number twenty-three. The front gate was missing, there was chipboard covering the front window and a burst black bin-bag spilling tea bags and empty bean tins outside the paint-stripped door.

Canner shrugged. 'Just what Smelly George told me, that's all.'

Lem blew out his breath. 'Only one way to find out,' he said. 'Kinard, can you go round the back in case he tries to leg it? The Can Man and I will be polite and knock.'

Kinard nodded and hurried away to climb over the fence. Lem and Canner gave him a couple of minutes and then made their way along the street.

'I've got a bad feeling about this,' Canner said.

Lem nodded. So had he. But he was sure his friend could figure that out for himself.

'Are we just going to appeal to his better side?' Canner asked. 'Just: "Please don't grass us up, Mr Riley, sir." Or do we threaten him? Maybe we should tie him up in a big sack, stamp him AIRMAIL and just chuck him on a plane back to that bloody awful country he came from.'

'Whatever it takes,' Lem said, scanning the street, glad there was no-one about.

'Do you knock on the door of a squat?' Canner wanted to know.

'Only if you're being polite,' Lem told him. He tried the handle. The door wasn't locked; it was half off its hinges, and his shoulder opened it easily enough.

It was dark and grimy in the hallway; all doors off it were

closed and the stairs rose up straight in front of them to another boarded-up window before turning back on themselves. They could smell rotten food. There were only a few tatty slivers of wallpaper left clinging to the walls; the rest was graffiti-daubed plaster. No carpet – just bare floorboards. Trash everywhere: beer cans, bottles, dead cigarettes, rags, ripped magazines and leaves. The warehouse really was a palace compared to this.

'Riley!' Lem shouted. 'We need to talk.'

They waited, but there wasn't a sound.

'Riley!'

Footsteps above them. They hurried up the stairs. Two doors led off the narrow landing. One was already open and inside they could see someone curled up on a bare mattress. Lem couldn't make out whether it was male or female at first, but then the girl rolled over towards them and he immediately recognised the look on her face. Sky high; away with the birds. He turned quickly away and thumped on the closed door.

'Riley! Riley, we need to talk.'

Canner kicked the door open.

The American was waiting for them, his ponytail greasier looking than ever, his grin somewhat forced. He was holding a radio. There were two piles of blankets on the bare floor, but his friend with the dragon tattoo wasn't around. A single sheet was drawn across one half of the window, yellowed net curtains covered the rest. The room was close, stagnant.

'Hey, visitors!' Riley said. He was close to the window, had maybe been about to make a break for it, but had been too late. However, he put on a good performance of nonchalance now. 'But yeah, you got me red-handed.' He held out the radio for them. 'I was just borrowing it, you know. Jan got it for me the other night. But I would've brought it back. No need for you guys to make the effort.'

Canner almost laughed. 'I didn't even know one had gone missing. Nicking one of our radios, now that really is low. Even for you.'

'You didn't know it was missing?' Riley clicked his fingers in a gosh-darn-it kind of way. 'Never did know when to keep my mouth shut.' He was acting as defiant as ever, but there was an edge to his voice and a flicker in his eye that betrayed the nerves underneath. It was obvious he hadn't been expecting to be found.

Lem took a step towards him, hoping the American would back away, but Riley stayed where he was.

'Funny you should mention keeping your mouth shut,' Lem said.

Riley watched him levelly. 'Your cheek looks sore, man. You ought to get a doctor to see to that for you.'

Lem ignored the jibe. 'I'm telling you to keep your mouth shut, now and for ever.'

'I don't know what you mean, Kingy. I'm sure you don't think—'

'Drop the act, Riley,' Canner told him.

Riley didn't take his eyes off Lem, but that traitorous flicker was getting stronger. 'Maybe you think I've got some sort of grudge against you and your kingdom. Maybe you think I've got it in for the whole hypocritical bullshit that goes on in there. Maybe you think—'

The walls of the room felt as though they were closing in on Lem, squeezing the air out so that he had to fight for breath.

'I just think you should keep your mouth shut.'

'But how're you gonna make sure I do that? You gonna beat me up, big guy?' He put on a posh English accent. 'Are you going to give me a jolly good thrashing? Well, I say!'

Lem was moving closer all the time, slowly crossing the room towards him, kicking the blankets aside. 'There's people in the warehouse who have nothing else. If it's closed down for whatever reason, they have nowhere else to go.'

'Unlike me who has the ever so enviable choice of this stinking pit or a shop doorway.'

'You had your chance in the warehouse.'

Riley sneered. 'I never broke your precious rule.'

'Maybe not, but there's people in that warehouse better off without you.'

Lem was within a metre of the American now, still meeting his stare, still moving closer. And at last Riley had to take a step back. Just a small step, almost as though he'd lost his balance for a second and simply had to alter his stance, but it was enough to let Lem know that he wasn't as tough as he liked to make out. That single step backwards told Lem he'd won.

So Lem backed the American all the way up against the wall without laying a single finger on him. He just forced him back so that he could feel the solid brick behind him and know there was nowhere else to go.

'We've found you this time, we can find you again.' He was feeling faint, could feel his lungs tightening, needing air, but he pushed his face close to the American's. 'Open your mouth just once, or pull one more of your stupid stunts, and Canner will find you. You've got my word.'

Riley's eyes had lost some of their defiance. Backed up against the wall his grin was not quite so sure. He squirmed and dodged away, but Canner was blocking the door. 'Trust me,' the Can Man told him, 'I'll find you wherever you go. I'll just follow your hamburger stench.'

'Maybe you should leave town just to be on the safe side,' Lem said. 'The further you are away the more difficult you are to find and the better for everybody.' He put his hand in his back pocket to feel his knife, but he pushed it back down.

He waited for Riley to drop his eyes first, then turned

quickly to leave. There was adrenaline pumping him up, making him clench his fists, grit his teeth. But it was also making his heart beat too fast with too little air. He'd won, though, right? No fists, no knife. Canner questioned him with a look, but he nodded. The scared, defeated look in the American's eyes had been enough. Now he just needed to get out and get some air.

They were on the stairs when Riley shouted from above, 'You're too late. Might as well prove what big men you are and beat me up now, because the deed's already been done.'

Canner turned to Lem, but Lem kept on down the stairs. He'd just won, hadn't he? This was the American simply trying to save face. Lem kept his fist clenched but didn't stop. He had to get some fresh air. His lungs were crying out for fresh air.

'Come and kick the crap out of me now, Kingy! I had a drink with a new security guard friend of mine last night. He was very interested in what I had to say.'

Kinard was at the bottom of the stairs. 'What's happened?'

'Let's just go,' Lem said.

They were back out on the street. Lem didn't stop walking but gulped in great lungfuls of air. He opened his mouth wide to suck them up.

'You okay?' Canner asked.

Lem could only nod. He wanted to be back in the warehouse.

'What if he's telling the truth?' Canner wanted to know.

Lem was panting like a dog. 'Then we're too late anyway.'

Six

Lem didn't bother to read to the end of *The Hunchback of Notre Dame*, and leaving a good book only half-read was something he hated doing. But he was worried it all ended badly for the poor hunchback.

He'd thought a lot about Riley's threat the other day, but was beginning to believe it less and less. The American was just trying to save face. He'd do the same if the tables were turned. Would he regret not trying to do something about it? He didn't know. How could he? He and Canner and Kinard had talked it over, and they'd all agreed there was nothing they could do except sit and wait and hope. He could still feel the ticking of that bomb, but it was muffled. With every day that passed it was getting easier to pretend it was just his watch.

And now Amy was leaving.

Canner would be following within the next few days. Soon Lem would be forced to stand on his own two feet, and he wasn't sure how capable they would be at supporting the rest of him. He was trying to decide what he was going to do, where he was going to go. He'd burned his bridges with his family and friends long ago – he couldn't expect them to be there for him. Maybe he should go abroad, he told himself. Australia, perhaps. As far as was humanly possible. He was terrified by the prospect of leaving the warehouse, so maybe going as far as he could – not just stretching the bond but snapping it completely – was the only answer.

They were gearing up for Canner's leaving party

downstairs: the kips were all weighed down with balloons and streamers. Trust the Can Man to make a fuss of himself. Everybody knew he wasn't actually going for a week or so yet, but he'd wanted to make a show while Amy was still around. He'd taken Robbie on one of his scavenging trips earlier, almost as an apprentice, to show him the secret of how it was done so that he could perhaps take over where Canner left off. It had been a successful first attempt by all accounts. 'Crisps and booze aplenty!' Canner had beamed.

He came up the stairs now and crossed the space to Lem's corner. 'You are coming to join in, aren't you?'

There was a ragged sticky-patch stuck over their friendship at the moment. Lem guessed it would heal properly given time. But he also knew there was so little time left. 'Maybe later,' he said.

'People are asking after you.'

'I don't fancy being around all that drink. Not in the mood I'm in at the minute.' It was a half-truth. Yes, it was tough being around drunks when you were sober – even tougher when you were desperate for a drink but scared it might start something up again. But really it was about having to look at a bunch of people he felt he was about to desert. He wondered why Canner didn't feel even a little twinge of the same.

'Can I ask you a question?'

The Can Man nodded. ''Course.'

'You've never told me what on earth you're going to do up there in Durham. How you're going to get by.'

'I'm staying with Amy at first, until I find something of my own. You know, I've got the kind of place I want in mind, but I'm guessing it's going to be tricky. But I'm the Can Man, right?' He smiled the widest smile possible. 'And Amy's going to ask her dad if he'll take me on at his estate agent's.'

Now Lem had heard it all. 'You're going to be an *estate agent*?'

Canner laughed. 'Well—'

But before he got chance to explain the shout went up: 'Patrol!'

As though they'd been trained, as though they'd been doing it most of their lives – which was how it felt – Lem went straight for the lights, killing their glow, while Canner was running for the stairs. Usually Lem wouldn't have followed him, but tonight was different. Tonight the warehouse had to be left safe – it was something he'd promised himself he'd do. If he was leaving this place, he was leaving it as he'd found it. Safe.

With the last light extinguished he ran towards the stairs in the gloom. He trailed his hand along the wall to guide him, not bothering about the sharp splinters, and followed the sound of Canner's voice below as he ordered lights and radios off. He descended the stairs into pitch blackness.

He could hear people running to and fro. 'Just get down and shut up,' Canner told them. There were several spy-holes cut into the far wall where someone could look out over the quayside road, to watch and wait for the security guards to move on. Lem guessed the Can Man would be at one of these, and he made his way over, skirting quickly but carefully round the kips in the dark. He had to hold out his hands in front of him to feel his way. Memory was no good because the kips were always changing, old ones falling down, new ones being hastily assembled.

He made it to the wall and found a spy-hole. He was about to crouch down to look when a sandy-haired head shoved its way in front: 'Canner?'

'Shhh! Something's not right.' Canner pushed past to another spy-hole further along.

'What is it?' Lem whispered. He put his eye to the hole

Canner had just left. Outside the evening light was fading. He could see the dusky road strewn with rubble, the quayside itself and the flat, black water. But he could only see straight ahead; the hole didn't allow for peripheral vision. He couldn't see any security guards. 'What's wrong?'

'There's only one guard, there's usually two.'

'That's good news, surely.'

Canner wasn't convinced. 'And I can't see what he's holding. A big water-carrier or something.'

'A what?'

'Like people have in caravans for water. It must be full because he's struggling with it.' He moved to yet another spy-hole. 'I don't get it.'

'Maybe he's coming for the party and it's full of booze.'

'I don't think either of us believe that now, do we?' Canner let his smile be heard. But it quickly evaporated as he pushed his eye back to the hole. 'The guards usually wander straight past, shine a torch up if they can be bothered. This guy's looking for something. He's—' He swore suddenly. 'He's heading for the side alley. He must know how to get inside.'

Lem's stomach turned cold. 'How?'

But Canner had gone.

Lem stayed still, silent. They hadn't mentioned Riley once. Of course they hadn't mentioned the American, because he'd been lying, right? But his words were haunting Lem now. They clicked and tapped, and finally ticked, inside his head.

He heard Canner's voice calling quietly for Kinard, telling him to get to the stairs. There was a mutter that rippled among the residents of Crap Palace: one or two came to see what they could at the spy-holes. They all knew something was going on. Then Kinard was crashing towards the stairs, evidently steam-rollering a few kips as he went. Canner told him to shut the hell up, but even Kinard's tiptoes were as heavy as a baby elephant's.

Lem scurried in the big lad's wake. One or two of the people he passed in the dark hissed questions at him, but he didn't have any answers himself. By the time he got to the door which led to the stairs below Kinard was crouched down holding it open. Lem could just make out the bulk of his shape in the shadows.

'The Can Man's downstairs,' he told Lem. He was holding the door open in case Canner needed to get back onto this floor quickly and silently. 'He said we should wait here.'

Lem nodded. Then whispered, 'Okay,' because he didn't think Kinard would have been able to see the nod.

'What's going on?' Kinard asked.

'Don't know. Canner seems to think a security guard is trying to get in.'

'But . . . No way.' Kinard wasn't going to believe that. 'He can't know where . . .' He stopped himself, then asked quietly: 'Riley's doing?'

Lem didn't answer. Kinard grunted.

A little shape ran up out of the darkness of the stairs towards them. It was Canner, breathing hard. 'He's inside,' he hissed. And there was real fear in his voice. The sound of it spooked Lem, because it was the first time he'd ever heard it in Canner. The Can Man didn't fear anything or anyone, did he?

'What do you want to do?' Kinard whispered. 'Do you want me to take him? I'll—'

'No, no. I want you to go get Robbie, as quick as you can.'

'What for?'

'I think it's his brother.'

The whispers were frantic, strained.

'What the hell . . .'

'It can't be. What the hell would he . . .'

'Just get Robbie, will you, Kinard? But for Christ's sake

don't tell anyone else what's happening, just tell them to keep quiet. And try not to sound like a herd of rhinos yourself.'

Lem watched the biggest shadow among them disappear. 'If you're right, and that's Robbie's brother down there, then—'

'I'm almost certain I'm right. Robbie's already told me his brother's a security guard. If Riley wasn't lying, if he *has* been talking to someone, it wouldn't be too hard for Frankie Hart to put two and two together, would it?' His silhouette shuffled awkwardly. 'I've messed up real bad this time, Lem. If we lose Crap Palace tonight it's all going to be my doing.'

The darkness of the warehouse was heavy around them. It was a weight on both their backs. They heard the gantry-style walkway which ran around the walls of the floor below creak with somebody's footsteps.

Canner swore through clenched teeth, his shadow flexed and grew as he strained to hold still. 'He even knows which set of stairs is safe to use,' he hissed. 'You've got to help me, Lem. Don't let me lose the warehouse. Not tonight. Not like this.'

Lem stared at the silhouette in front of him, desperate to find his old ally's face. It was the first time the Can Man had ever asked for his help. 'Not tonight,' he promised.

Kinard and Robbie appeared out of the darkness. Canner waved his hands about dramatically to keep them quiet and show them where he was. Lem gently, silently pulled the door to the stairs closed. 'Kinard,' he whispered urgently, 'can you hold this door closed? Make it seem like it's locked.'

Kinard had sense enough not to ask questions. He shouldered in between them and took up a braced stance in front of the door, with his hands pulling back on the push bar that opened it.

Then they waited.

They searched the darkness for each other's faces, as they

strained their ears to listen. There was no doubting somebody was out there. All hearts were in throats, thumping away. There was a fumbling at the door and all eyes flicked to Kinard's shadow, but he didn't budge an inch. The door rattled stiffly, quietly. Kinard didn't move. No-one breathed.

After about a minute they heard the intruder sneak away again, but nobody moved for two or three minutes more. When Canner finally stood up the rest of them started back in surprise. Lem's muscles, which had been stretched tense, slowly eased, tingling with pins and needles as the blood returned.

'Let's make sure he's gone,' the Can Man whispered. Kinard stepped aside, but when Canner pushed gently at the door it wouldn't open. He put his shoulder to it. The push bar flapped uselessly up and down.

'Let me try.' But it wouldn't yield even to Kinard's massive shoulders. 'He's locked us in. How's he done that?' He heaved his full weight at the door, shaking it on its hinges, but could not open it a millimetre more.

'A couple of wedges in the gap at the bottom should be enough,' Lem said. He was frightened now. This door was the only exit from the warehouse. If that was Frankie Hart out there then Lem already knew what kind of person he was, and he remembered the threats he'd shouted. But what exactly did he want them locked in for? Was he going to fetch other guards . . . the police?

Kinard was slamming himself into the door. Canner was taking Robbie to a spy-hole to see if it really was his brother. Lem remembered what Canner had said about the guard struggling to carry something. A heavy water-carrier, wasn't it? He was the first to smell smoke.

Not water. Petrol.

SEVEN

'Get that door open!' he shouted at Kinard. 'Smash it off its hinges if you have to.' He searched the darkness for Canner. 'Turn the lights on!' he shouted. 'We need lights on. Now!'

Slowly the inside of the warehouse was illuminated by its usual orange glow. Blurred anxious faces emerged from the kips – everybody knew something was wrong, but no-one knew exactly what. They all turned to him, questioning him. And already there were tails of smoke curling up through the cracks in the wooden floor. Lem saw the slow realisation dawn on a young girl's face. She screamed.

And everybody was shouting, everybody was running.

Why fire? Lem thought. Why's it have to be fire?

'Keep back!' Canner yelled. He and Robbie did what they could to hold everybody back. 'Give them room.'

Lem could tell that Kinard was tiring as he slammed and slammed against the door. 'We need a battering ram,' he said. He shouted at Robbie: 'We need a battering ram!'

Robbie nodded and pushed his way through the crowd. Canner lashed out at a few people, yelling at them to let him through.

Lem's mind hurtled, desperate to keep pace with his hammering heart. The smell of smoke was getting stronger by the second. Robbie was at the nearest kip, made of lean-to doors. Lem pushed through the crowd and between them they pulled it apart. Then he and Kinard used two doors nailed flat together as their battering ram. They aimed low at the jammed door.

Lem thought briefly of his corner upstairs – his books and his desk and the time he'd spent up there the past year. It was all going to disappear in flames. Maybe they could get water from the docks to put the fire out? But what would they carry it in? And how do you throw buckets of water at a three-storey building the length of a football pitch? No, it was all going to go. The desk and the notepads full of his writing too.

The thick smoke rising through the orange glow of the lights looked like poison gas in a scary movie. And it so easily could have been, because people were coughing and choking all around him now. Nerves were frayed raw. 'This time,' he yelled at Kinard. 'It has to be this time.'

With a bellow they charged at the door with their makeshift battering ram. And the wood splintered and crunched and gave way as its hinges burst. More smoke poured in.

Lem jumped down the stairs and through the door onto the walkway. The floor below was alive with flames. Robbie's brother couldn't have had all that much petrol, but the old beams, dusty and dry after the long hot summer, were rushing the fire along. It was the noise that surprised him. The fire was so loud. Like hundreds of gunshots as the wood cracked open under the pressure and the heat – the heat that was rolling over him in waves. It was the most frightening sensation he'd ever felt.

He ran back up the short stairs. 'Take them down,' he shouted at Kinard. 'You lead them out.' Then he and Canner stepped aside to let people through. They pushed and shoved against each other. 'Don't push. Give everyone a chance.'

Amy was with Canner. 'Is that everybody?' she shouted over the commotion. 'How many were in tonight?'

'I don't know.' Lem grabbed Canner's arm. 'How many in tonight? How many?'

Canner's face was tight, frightened. 'How should I know? Thirty, maybe thirty-five. It's not as though we keep a frigging register!'

'We've got to check the kips,' Robbie said.

'Surely nobody could be sleeping through this.'

Lem and Canner stared hard at one another. No decision they'd ever made before had meant life or death.

'You two get going,' Lem said to Robbie and Amy.

'Go!' Canner told them. 'We'll check.'

They started shouting through the smoke, hurrying between the kips. They had to hold their T-shirts over their mouths. The heat was enough to burst the balloons for Canner's party and the streamers curled and blackened. The curtains on Amy and Shelly's kip went up with a whoomph.

Lem's face was streaked with black, his eyes stinging, watering in the heat. 'Not tonight,' he'd promised Canner.

A huge rending sound filled the air. A cracking and splitting. And then screams. Lem knew instantly what had happened. He ran back to the stairs, Canner behind him. Robbie and Amy clutched at each other, staring at the nightmare below. The gantry-style walkway had collapsed under the weight of people.

Canner grabbed Amy. 'Are you all right? *Are you all right?*'

Lem knew they were trapped up here. The dark world below was stuttering images in hot orange and red and yellow as the flames lit random patches of the ground floor. The fire reached up, groping higher, higher. The floor burned. The walls burned. The smoke billowed up into his face, filling his throat with ash, stabbing needles of heat into his eyes. He watched from above as people ran stumbling or were carried towards the door to the alleyway. They seemed careless of the burning floor, the burning walls. They dragged each other through the flames, slapping frantically at clothes and hair. Lem closed his eyes and hoped with his whole life that

Robbie's brother hadn't barred that door as well. The old warehouse creaked and groaned. It wouldn't last long. But with a screech of metal that was barely audible above the conflagration the door to safety was pulled open and everybody started flooding outside.

Except them.

'How do we get down?' Robbie asked. The remains of the walkway lay broken on the ground below them, smoking, then catching the flames.

'Lower yourselves to me.' Kinard was down there, reaching up to them. As his bulk flickered and danced in the shadows thrown by the fire Lem could see the blood on his face and the nasty burned patch of missing hair.

Canner went first, then he could help Kinard lower the rest of them from below. He dropped most of the way, twisting his ankle beneath him. Kinard had blood in his eyes and tried to wipe it away.

Amy followed. Lem could feel her trembling as he and Robbie lowered her over the edge. 'We've got you,' he told her. 'You're okay.' She got down safely and Canner immediately shoved her towards the door.

Robbie next. But Lem was frightened, impatient. Fire scared him so badly. The heat on his face was painful. He didn't wait for help but turned round to grab hold of whatever he could to lower himself as quickly as possible. The skin of his fingertips blistered on the hot wood, but Kinard grabbed him safely enough when he dropped.

Then they were dodging the flames as they ran to the door, up the alleyway and out onto the quayside. The group of people huddled there were bloody and smoke-blackened but so very pale underneath.

'Is everybody here?' Lem asked. 'Anybody know if anyone's still inside?'

There was a dazed shaking of heads.

'Where's Stef?' Canner wanted to know.

'She's working,' Shelly told him. 'Ain't *she* gonna be surprised when she gets back.'

Nobody talked; everybody watched silently. Lem held his blistered hands under his arms in an attempt to ease the pain. But it was inside that it hurt the most.

'Look!' somebody said, pointing down the road towards the rusty cranes.

A small Securicor van had its headlights on full beam to pick out a guard standing in front. He shouted something at them, but the abuse was lost over the noise of the dying warehouse.

Lem looked at Robbie, who nodded once. Frank.

'Maybe Kinard should pay Riley another visit,' Canner said.

But Lem could only shrug.

Sirens rose and fell in the distance. The fire brigade was on its way. They wouldn't be able to save the warehouse, but they'd have to stop the fire from spreading through the rest of the docks. The breeze was scattering deadly embers.

'We better get going,' Kinard said.

'Where?' Shelly asked.

Kinard didn't have an answer.

And everybody looked to Lem. They turned towards him, moving to close ranks around him. All eyes were on him, looking for the answer.

'I've got nowhere else to go,' someone said.

'I can't go home,' said another.

'I've got nowhere else to go.'

'There isn't anywhere.'

There was a second panic in the air now, a fluttering, bird-like fear flitting between this scruffy group of misfits, runaways and strays. Lem could feel it too. He couldn't help wondering what would have happened to him if Canner hadn't been there. Or what would have happened to Robbie when his brother went off the rails if Lem himself hadn't been there.

He couldn't help wondering what was going to happen to the rest of them.

He guessed they were going to end up in stinking squats like Riley – places which really did make the warehouse look like a palace. It was a disturbing, dispiriting thought. The image of the girl on the mattress was suddenly horribly vivid in his mind and he stared hard at the flames in an attempt to burn the memory away.

Canner was at his shoulder. 'I never told you what I was going to do in Durham,' he said. 'I'm going to set up another warehouse. I just need to find the right place. But that's what I'm going to do: Durham's version of Crap Palace.'

Lem nodded, turned away from the fire. 'I didn't think being an estate agent was really going to be your thing.'

'Guess not,' Canner admitted. 'But it's kind of close, if you think about it.'

'Kind of,' Lem agreed. 'And because I'm king, you're going to be doing your utmost to convince me Durham is just another part of my kingdom.'

Canner gave a single, emphatic nod. 'Damn right.'

The original Crap Palace groaned as its floors crashed down, its walls fell inward. Lem's palace rolled over to die. He was homeless too. The black smoke was enough to choke the night sky. The building seemed to shriek as it burned, sounding to Lem like it was crying out as the flames engulfed its old wooden heart. He knew he was lost without it.

He turned to Kinard, who immediately stepped forward as if coming to attention, ready to take an order or follow a request. And when he looked to Robbie, the younger lad did exactly the same. Which was reassuring. Because he was going to need all the help he could get.

He'd not yet learned enough – he certainly wasn't sure enough, and had no idea how it was all going to end, but . . .

'One last request before you leave,' he said quietly to the Can Man. 'Can you find me another warehouse? Bigger, safer, for whoever else may need to come?'

Canner smiled slowly, his grin widening, stretching. 'Of *course* I can,' he said, sounding slightly offended that it had ever been in doubt.

BIG thanks
to Charlie who's worked just as hard as I have. To Carolyn for more patience than I sometimes deserve. To Julie and Matilda for long phone calls (usually my bill) and advice. To Mum, Dad and John for all their support. Also to Steve and Nicky – as ever. And not forgetting Hannah. Never forgetting Hannah.